The Other Face

The Other Face

Barbara C. Freeman

with decorations by the author

E. P. DUTTON & CO., INC.   NEW YORK

First published in the U.S.A. 1976 by E. P. Dutton
Copyright © 1975 by Barbara C. Freeman

Library of Congress Cataloging in Publication Data

Freeman, Barbara Constance   The other face

SUMMARY: In the long line of distinctive Dovewood
faces, another face occasionally appears. Betony has
that other face and unlocks its mystery when she finds
an old china knick-knack.

[1. Space and time—Fiction.   2. England—Social life
and customs—19th century—Fiction]   I. Title.

PZ7.F8746Ot4   [Fic]   76-19057   ISBN 0-525-36453-6

Printed in the U.S.A.   First Edition
10 9 8 7 6 5 4 3 2 1

Contents

Betony

I

The Red Cloak

"I recognised you at once," said Linny. "I said to Gerard, 'There she is,' and he said, 'Where?' and I said, 'Over there,' and he said, 'That girl's not Betony,' and I said, 'Not that one – the one in the red cloak, she's got the other face,' and Gerard said, 'Well, we'd better ask her.' And we did. And you were."

The taxi swerved out of the station yard. "I ought to have told you I'd be wearing my school cloak," said Betony.

"It's beautiful," said Linny. "It's fantastic."

"I shouldn't really be wearing it, because I left school

in the summer," said Betony, "but I'd no winter coat."

"Why didn't the Great Aunts give you one?" said Linny.

"They didn't think of it," said Betony. "And everything was arranged so quickly."

"I wish I could go to school in a red cloak," said Linny.

"It's only a uniform," said Betony. "When the school was started most country girls wore red cloaks." And the conversation died.

"Today is early closing, so Spurrey has gone down to the river," said Gerard at last.

"Spurrey?" said Betony.

"Grandfather – yours and ours," said Gerard. "I feel I should make you a speech of welcome since this is the first time we've met."

"Yes," said Betony.

"You seem to have been leading a rather extraordinary life, with the old Aunts."

"Yes," said Betony. "I didn't know you called Grandfather 'Spurrey'."

"Everybody does," said Gerard. "It *is* his name, you know."

"Yes," said Betony.

"I sometimes wonder what mad horticulturalist began all the plant names in the family," said Gerard. "I'm always thankful that Mother found Herb Gerard for me. Don't look so startled. I'm only making conversation."

"Yes," said Betony.

"You're a girl of few words, aren't you?" said Gerard.

"I'm afraid I'm not much good at conversation," said Betony.

The taxi jerked to a stop at the traffic lights.

"But don't you talk to the Great Aunts?" said Linny.

"No," said Betony.

"But don't they talk to you?"

"No," said Betony. "But they tell me what to do."

"Do they talk to each other all the time then?" said Linny.

"No," said Betony. She hesitated.

"They've not spoken to each other for the last three years," she said. "I – I carry messages."

"I'm not surprised that the doctor said you had to get away," said Gerard, and there was another painful silence.

"You mustn't think I'm ill," said Betony, "but I couldn't stop worrying. And I kept bursting into tears. It annoyed the Aunts."

"Of course they quarrelled with Spurrey years ago," said Gerard. "We've never seen them."

"I know," said Betony.

"Tell us about them," said Linny.

The traffic lights changed and the taxi shot forward.

"Well—" said Betony. "Well—"

"What are they like?" said Linny.

"Well," said Betony, "Aunt May is the elder. She has white hair and a deep voice. And she rests in her room between meals."

"And what does she do?"

"Well," said Betony, "she has an electric kettle and makes herself cups of tea. And she eats biscuits because she thinks the Fire of Life may go out if it isn't constantly stoked. And she wears a hat because she's afraid of earache. But she's very dignified."

"D'you mean that she wears a hat in the house?" said Linny.

"Well, yes," said Betony. "She never goes out."

"And Aunt Maple?" said Gerard.

"Well," said Betony, "well – she has red hair and she's very thin. And she paints the family photos. There are five albums and she's nearly finished the third. She gives

9

all the Dovewoods bright pink cheeks and – and rainbow-coloured clothes."

"Why does she do that?" asked Linny.

Betony was staring out of the window. "I suppose she thinks she's doing them a kindness," she said. "She makes them all look very healthy."

"But aren't they all dead?" said Linny.

"Yes," said Betony.

"I don't think I should like the Aunts," said Linny.

"Two twopence-coloured old eccentrics," said Gerard.

"They're Dovewoods," said Betony as though that explained everything.

The taxi swept round a corner.

"Well, you'll find Spurrey relatively harmless," said Gerard. "We often stay with him when the parents are away filming."

"Yes," said Betony.

"Of course Spurrey's hopeless as a shopkeeper," said Gerard. "He's been painting snowstorms all the summer. He's gone down to the river this afternoon. It's early closing today."

"Yes," said Betony.

"But what do *you* do?" asked Linny.

"I've been running Dovewood House since I left school," said Betony. "The Aunts have a temporary housekeeper at the moment but she'll only stay for a few weeks. We once had seven housekeepers in one year. It's always like that."

"I'm not surprised," said Gerard.

The taxi was slowing down and the street lights had come on.

"This is Albert Terrace," said Gerard. "And here's Number 26. I don't expect you remember it."

"But I do," said Betony. "It's hardly changed at all."

The taxi stopped.

"We have to go through the shop now to get into the house," said Linny. "Once, when Spurrey wanted some money, he sold the front door and part of the hall to the shop next door."

"I'll see to your suitcase," said Gerard.

2

No. 26

The sign over the shop said *S. Dovewood – Art Repository.* In the window was a miscellaneous jumble of coloured inks and paints, small picture-frames, chalks and paintbrushes. Old prints hung at the back of the window, and several strands of tinsel, the only concession to the Christmas season, were suspended between views of the Thames, St Paul's Cathedral and Temple Bar.

It was clear that S. Dovewood was totally uninterested in the art of window-dressing.

To Betony, staring through the frosty glass, it seemed that thirteen desperate and unhappy years had been, for an instant, swept away.

Gerard opened the door and the shop bell jangled furiously.

"Spurrey hates that bell," said Linny.

Gerard switched on a light, and Betony looked about her. "I remember all this," she said. "I stayed here before – before I went to Dovewood House."

The counter was on the left and the walls were hidden by overcrowded shelves. A great Victorian wardrobe and a high cupboard, set side by side, cut off the far end of the shop. There was a picture-postcard stand behind the shop window and a forest of easels in one corner.

On the chair by the counter were two large, shabby shoes and a black umbrella.

"Only those weren't there before," said Betony.

"Spurrey's gone out in his slippers again," said Gerard.

"Mrs O'Connor always tries to remind him to change," said Linny, "but he never remembers."

"Mrs O'Connor?" said Betony.

"She comes in, in the mornings, to cook Spurrey's lunch and do a bit of housework," said Gerard. "She saw him eating bread and cheese in the shop one day when she had rushed in to buy a flowery calendar. Mrs O'Connor's like that."

"There used to be a tray of purses on the counter," said Betony. "And one day . . . Spurrey . . . suddenly said that I might choose a present – anything I liked. And I chose a blue purse; I still have it."

"Spurrey must have had one of his Giving Away days," said Linny. "D'you know that you look terribly pale?"

"I usually do," said Betony.

"I'll go and put the kettle on," said Gerard. "It's no good waiting for Spurrey. The kitchen and parlour are down in the basement and we sleep at the top of the house. Your room's up there too. Linny will show you the way. Spurrey's bedroom is on the floor below, next to the big drawing-room which hasn't been used since Granny died. You have to go through that door behind the counter. Don't fall over the boxes in the hall."

The passage at the top of the house was roofed by a huge skylight, and there were three closed doors.

Linny opened the nearest door.

"Don't come in for a moment," she said.

Betony stood still.

She remembered the passage, she remembered the skylight and she remembered sitting on the top stair and spreading out the six pennies that her grandmother had given her to put in the blue purse. The telephone, ringing far below in the hall, had broken across the silence of that summer afternoon.

Suddenly Betony was overwhelmed by the old, anguished sense of loss.

There had been a period of total bewilderment when everyone had been very kind. There had been a journey. Then Great Aunt Maple had closed the door of Dovewood House behind her, and Great Aunt May had swept down the stairs booming, "So this is Betony! No tears, I hope. We can't have cry-babies here."

After that, for weeks, the child had watched for her mother and father to come and take her home. Later, much later, she accepted the fact that they would never come. To Betony, it seemed that all her happiness had ended abruptly, when she was four years old.

"You may come in now," said Linny. "I only wanted to switch on the fire."

The room was festooned with tinsel and hung with pink and silver Christmas tree balls. Sprigs of holly and mistletoe lay along the edge of the mantelpiece and there was a single Christmas rose in a tumbler by the bed.

"We found the flower in the garden," said Linny. "We made you a special room, so you wouldn't feel homesick. I said to Gerard, 'I've got fifteen pennies left,' and Gerard said—"

"I shan't feel homesick," said Betony.

"D'you know I can work magic?" said Linny. "I said to myself this morning, 'If I can get to the bus stop in seven steps – then Betony will come. But if I can't – then the old Aunts will keep her for ever.' And my last step was enormous and I bumped into the fat lady at the end of the queue. But she was quite nice when I explained. And here you are."

"Yes," said Betony. "Here I am."

Gerard came in with the suitcase and set it down by the bed.

"I hope you've brought plenty of warm clothes," he said. "You'll need them in this house."

"I'm used to the cold," said Betony. "I'm not allowed a fire in my room at Dovewood House."

"Like the Jane Austen girl," said Gerard.

"She got a fire in the end," said Betony. She turned and walked to the window. It overlooked the garden, a wilderness of frosty grass and unpruned apple trees, already darkening in the winter twilight.

"You mustn't be too kind to me," said Betony. "You're Dovewoods and so am I, but I'm not a typical Dovewood. I've no personality. I'm so – so – colourless that I sometimes feel I'm invisible – a kind of ghost. I've probably been a ghost for years. Ever since I went to Dovewood House."

Behind her the small glittering room was growing warm but she continued to stare into the dusk.

"In a few weeks I shall have to go back to Dovewood House," she said, "so you mustn't be too kind to me. I'm not used to it."

"Oh well!" said Gerard. "The kettle's probably boiling. Come down when you're ready."

3

Spurrey

The parlour was firelit and shabby. It opened into an "area", an enclosed space which was lighted by thick glass let into the pavement above. Shadowy feet crossed and re-crossed the glass, and the street lamp outside Number 26 illuminated the area with a faint, melancholy light.

Gerard was making toast.

"We reminded Spurrey that you were coming today," he said, "but he's probably forgotton. He doesn't bother about anything much these days except his painting. The shop is a dead loss. Luckily he has three old cottages, in River Walk, that belonged to Granny. We live in the largest of them. I suppose you don't mind if Linny pours out. It's one of her childish pleasures."

"No," said Betony. "I don't mind."

Linny switched on the light and drew the curtains.

They had almost finished tea when a black and white cat stalked into the room, glanced round and stalked out again.

"That was Curzon," said Linny. "He's looking for Spurrey."

"Curzon moved in about a year ago," said Gerard. "No one claimed him and so he stayed. He's extremely anti-social. He spends most of his time on top of the cupboard in the shop. He enjoys looking down on Spurrey's customers. He's that kind of cat."

"Spurrey keeps a pair of steps at the back of the cupboard so that Curzon can climb up and down when he wants to," said Linny.

"The Aunts don't approve of animals," said Betony. "So I've never known a cat."

Spurrey appeared as the clock was striking half past five. He was tall and stooping, with a thin beard and dark hair that curled over his coat collar. He wore a yellow muffler and ancient slippers.

He looked at Betony.

"But I thought you were keeping house for my two formidable sisters," he said.

"I was," said Betony. "But—"

"Ah, yes," said Spurrey. "I knew that I'd made a mental note of something but I couldn't recollect what it was."

He shook hands.

"May wrote to me, in her usual peremptory style," he said. "And Maple wrote by the same post. They announced that you'd be paying us a visit."

He paused, staring vaguely at the jam.

"They quarrelled with me years ago," he said. "It was when I married."

"I'll make some more tea," said Gerard.

Spurrey began to unwind his yellow muffler.

"The Dovewoods were once a united family," he said. "Most of the Victorian Dovewoods were shopkeepers, of one sort or another, but they were always a little eccentric. Of course, they made money – some of them – and those who didn't were regarded with slight disapproval. But they were a united family. And they loved the arts. Some were quite good photographers."

"Hadn't you better take off your overcoat?" said Linny.

"They photographed each other on every possible occasion," said Spurrey. "At weddings and baptisms and

17

funerals. They photographed each other outside their shops or sitting by the sea. And we each have a set of the five great albums. But then the family began to dwindle."

"Do take off your coat," said Linny.

"And the eccentricity increased," said Spurrey. "Old Rowan Dovewood lived alone, in Dovewood House, for fifty years, and seems to have spent his time french-polishing the furniture. He left the house, and all his money, to May and Maple, and I thought, at the time, that it was the most sensible thing he ever did. But now I'm not so sure. I thought it would end the old feuds between them but it seems I was wrong." He began to take off his overcoat but paused.

"How are my two intimidating sisters?" he said. "It's many years since I was last received at Dovewood House. May, I remember, wore a purple velvet hat to carve the beef. And Maple's hair was a curious shade of yellow ochre."

"Betony says Aunt Maple's hair is red now," said Linny.

"Ah!" said Spurrey. "That was always the trouble. Maple could never leave things alone. She always knew better than Nature. And May detested change. So they were always at loggerheads."

"They lead their separate lives now," said Betony.

"And you?" said Spurrey. "Do you lead a separate life too? Whenever I wrote to enquire I was informed that you were well and happy. And whenever I wrote direct to you your replies were so brief – but you too said that you were happy."

"I know," said Betony. "It didn't seem right to – to complain when the Aunts had given me a home."

"I take it that neither May nor Maple was particularly observant," said Spurrey and hung his coat over the back of the chair.

"I disappointed the Aunts," said Betony. "Aunt May used to tell me I'd no personality. And Aunt Maple said I'd no imagination. And they were right. They expected me to do great things at school – because I was a Dovewood. And I didn't shine at all. That's why they wouldn't let me stay on."

"They'll probably miss you more than they'll ever admit," said Spurrey.

"They'll miss an unpaid housekeeper," said Betony. "A housekeeper who won't give notice."

Then Gerard came back with the tea.

"If you're writing to Dovewood House," said Spurrey, "perhaps you'll tell my sisters that they'll be welcome here at any time – if they'd like to come and see you. I know it would mean something of a journey for them but—"

"Yes," said Betony. "I'll tell them."

4

Mrs O'Connor

The next morning was foggy and very cold. Gerard and Linny started for school early. Betony washed the breakfast things and then followed Spurrey up into the shop. She found him flicking vaguely at the counter with a duster.

"Is there anything I can do?" she said.

"Nothing, nothing," said Spurrey. "I leave the house to Mrs O'Connor. She likes to think she's indispensable and I never argue with her. But I don't let her touch the shop. I forgot to ask if you'd slept well."

"I dreamed that the Aunts were hiding under Temple Bar," said Betony. "They were waiting to take me back to Dovewood House. I suppose it was that old print in the window that—"

Then the shop bell jangled and Mrs O'Connor appeared.

She was brisk and small. She had sharp brown eyes and a sharp, high-bridged nose. She shut the door and put down her basket.

"Good morning," she said. "So you're Betony! I'm glad you've arrived. Linaria was afraid the old aunts would chain you in the cellar. There's ice on the step, Mr Spurrey. Your customers will be falling about like ninepins if you don't put down some sand."

"I doubt if there'll be many customers this morning," said Spurrey. "Can you spare a moment, Mrs O'Connor? How's the fog?"

"Nasty," said Mrs O'Connor. "And as to sparing a

moment – they'll be your moments I'm sparing. I suppose you're still fussing with all that snow?"

"Yes," said Spurrey.

Mrs O'Connor glanced at Betony. "You're too thin and too pale," she said. "Come along! We'd better see what your grandfather's been up to."

The space behind the wardrobe and the cupboard was lighted by a tall window and warmed by an oil stove. The furniture consisted of an easel and a table, a chair, a pair of steps and Curzon. Curzon was sitting on the table among piles of water-colours. He hissed softly when he saw Mrs O'Connor, sprang for the steps and vanished on the top of the cupboard.

"I can't think how you put up with that cat," said Mrs O'Connor. "I've never known a more stand-offish creature."

"Well," said Spurrey, "he puts up with me."

Mrs O'Connor stationed herself in front of the easel. She was silent for several seconds.

"Now that's what I call real snow," she said at last. "Very nasty weather, if I may say so."

"You may," said Spurrey. "You may."

"You can see there's a lot more to come," said Mrs O'Connor.

Betony said nothing.

Spurrey had painted a wood lashed by a driving white storm, and she seemed to feel the deathly cold. Yet when she looked closer there were nothing but long streaks and patches of grey, dried trickles of paint and fierce brush strokes.

"What's that man doing out of doors in such dreadful weather?" said Mrs O'Connor.

It wasn't all just snow. There was someone there, in the cold, braced against the wind, waiting.

"I needed that touch of sepia," said Spurrey.

"But what's he *doing*?" said Mrs O'Connor.

"I suppose he's a traveller," said Spurrey.

"Well, he won't get far in that storm," said Mrs O'Connor. "Is that a cloak he's wearing?"

"He's waiting for the stage-coach," said Spurrey. "Yes, that's it. But the last stage-coach has gone, Mrs O'Connor, and railways have come, and monstrous planes. And men have landed on the moon. But the wood has grown up round him and he still waits and waits. What else can he do?"

"A macabre bit of nonsense," said Mrs O'Connor. "It's time I was getting on with my work. I'll be losing all my toes with frostbite if I look at that wood of yours much longer. Why don't you paint something cheerful for a change? A nice garden, perhaps, with roses and a sun-dial?"

"I'll bear it in mind," said Spurrey.

Mrs O'Connor retreated.

"A worthy citizen," said Spurrey. "A very worthy citizen."

"Yes," said Betony.

"People are extremely kind," said Spurrey. "They come into the shop and talk to me. They tell me the most extraordinary things. And they bring me books and home-made jam. But I still expect that your grandmother will one day open the door behind the counter and put down a cup of tea for me and a slice of cold bread pudding. I always liked her bread puddings. She made one every week. She was ill for a long time, you know. Your voice is a little like hers – I thought so last night."

Curzon peered down from the top of the cupboard and began cautiously to descend. He hesitated and then leapt for the table.

"Of course Gerard is a tower of strength," said

Spurrey. "He knows all the answers and speaks with the magisterial assurance of seventeen. And, as for Linny, she's a child of imagination, I'm always glad when they move in with me."

"Yes," said Betony. "I can understand that."

"But there are the other times," said Spurrey. "The times in between."

"Yes," said Betony.

She was still staring at the man in the snow.

"I try to occupy myself," said Spurrey. "But time itself is the problem. I never had enough time when your grandmother was here. But now an hour can be like a day. It's a rum go. And clocks have nothing to do with it. We should have kept you if your grandmother had not been ill."

"Yes," said Betony. "I know that. It's one of the few things I do know. I'll go and find some sand for the step. And then may I look round the shop?"

"You may," said Spurrey. "You may."

Later in the morning the sun, small, silvery and still half lost in fog, appeared briefly over Albert Terrace. Mrs O'Connor opened the door behind the counter and said, "I'm off now."

"Yes, Mrs O'Connor," said Betony.

"I see you've taken over the shop," said Mrs O'Connor.

"I've been looking round," said Betony.

"Lunch is in the oven. Ready in twenty minutes. See you have a proper meal," said Mrs O'Connor.

"Yes," said Betony.

"You're underweight," said Mrs O'Connor. "And you needn't argue about it. I'm a state-registered nurse and I use my eyes."

"I wasn't arguing," said Betony.

"I gave up nursing for matrimony," said Mrs

O'Connor. "And then matrimony gave me up. Never marry a bookmaker with a heart condition."

"I won't," said Betony.

"He's dead now," said Mrs O'Connor. "He was twenty years older than I was, but we were comfortable enough together. He left me a nice little nest egg and that's why I'm here. I didn't want to go back to nursing but I do like to be useful. Of course your grandfather has his little ways but I jolly him along. He'd never eat a hot meal or buy a new pair of shoes if I weren't here. I always say if you can't be useful in this world where can you be useful?"

"I don't know," said Betony.

"Of course I'd like to get my hands on the garden," said Mrs O'Connor. "That's what I'd really like. But he says he prefers a jungle. I've got a flat – all mod cons but no garden – and I still miss the garden we had when we were kids. I dream about it sometimes. Now why am I telling you all this? You must be a good listener. If you want something to do this afternoon you might tidy the big cupboard over there and make room for the boxes in the hall. I'm sick of falling over them."

"I do want something to do," said Betony.

"It'll be a miracle if he let's you touch the cupboard," said Mrs O'Connor. "Oh, well! I must be getting along. I don't want to get lost in the fog. See you tomorrow."

The shop bell jangled and she was gone.

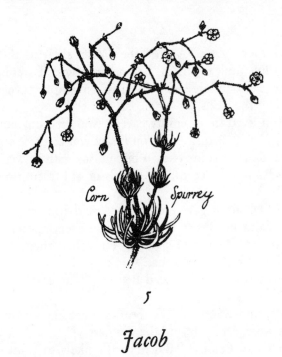

Corn Spurrey

5

Jacob

By two o'clock the sun had vanished and the fog had thickened. Betony made up the parlour fire and returned to the shop. Spurrey had retreated to his hidden painting room. Betony edged round the corner of the great wardrobe.

"I need something to do," she said. "May I tidy the cupboard?"

"It's full," said Spurrey. "I locked the doors because things kept falling out. Your grandmother could keep them in order but I can't. They accumulate and accumulate."

"I've noticed that they've accumulated in the shop," said Betony.

"Your grandmother packed the three top shelves of the cupboard years ago," said Spurrey. "And I've not

25

touched them since. As for the lower shelves, there's nothing but junk on them. I sometimes wish I were one of those early fellows who lived in an empty cave and painted on the walls."

"If you lived in an empty cave it wouldn't stay empty for long," said Betony. "D'you know you've three separate collections of compasses in biscuit-tins with flowers on the lids? And you've rolls and rolls of old tracing paper and—"

"Mrs O'Connor gave me the tins," said Spurrey. "I get biscuits from her every Christmas and every Easter. She can never resist roses or pansies. Though perhaps I *may* get a violet tin this Christmas."

"You've one already," said Betony. "There are scissors in it."

"Ah," said Spurrey. "I'd been wondering where the scissors were. Did you find the sunglasses?"

"No," said Betony. "But nobody's likely to want sunglasses in this fog."

"You can never tell what the public will want," said Spurrey. "I get infants in here demanding lollies and schoolgirls who want pop records. And only last Monday a wretched youth asked for house-painters' brushes. He said he was decorating a flat for his father. Mrs O'Connor shooed him out of the shop because my dinner was ready. I've just remembered – I don't stock sunglasses any longer."

"Why was the youth wretched?" asked Betony.

"He gave that impression," said Spurrey vaguely. "He'd a slight stammer but I think he'd have liked to stay and talk. It struck me afterwards that I might have offered him some of Mrs O'Connor's cauliflower cheese – only she never puts enough cheese on the top. Your grandmother knew exactly how I liked it. I'd better switch the lights on."

The fog had invaded the shop. A milky haze blurred the outlines of the shelves and the innumerable boxes everywhere. The electric lights were isolated, each in its own halo.

"What's the other face?" said Betony. "Linny said I had it, but I don't know what it is."

"Haven't you ever looked at the family albums?" said Spurrey. "Most of the Dovewoods have blue eyes, fair hair and the prominent Dovewood chin. It's extraordinary how that chin appears in generation after generation. But another type of face crops up occasionally – a face with a different bone structure and dark eyes. And you have that type of face. I've often wondered where it came from. Of course there were variations but—"

"I see," said Betony.

The shop bell clanged and a stout woman peered into the shop.

"Do you sell—?" she began, and then, "Oh, I see you don't. I'm so sorry. It's this fog." She retreated precipitately and the bell quavered into silence.

"I must find *something* to do," said Betony. "I don't really feel I'm here yet. I'm almost afraid I shall float away in the fog."

"Tidy the cupboard then. I'll bring you the steps," said Spurrey. "And if anyone comes into the shop—"

"I'll say you're coping with another snowfall," said Betony.

The cupboard doors had been forced shut.

As Betony turned the key the doors burst open and piles of picture-postcards, boxes of paperclips and a mixed collection of gloves cascaded to the floor. The paperclips were rusty and the gloves all odd. And the picture-postcards, Betony guessed, were sixty or seventy years old. They were local views – of the river and the church, of the first wooden railway station, of the Assembly Rooms and Albert Terrace.

Betony spread a few of them on the counter. She packed the rest into an empty biscuit-tin with poppies on the lid.

Then she fetched a brush and dustpan and knelt to sweep up the paperclips.

And suddenly it seemed that she was back at Dovewood House, kneeling to replace the brass fire-irons in the library grate. And Aunt Maple was stooped over the albums on the polished table.

"Brightness and health go hand in hand," said Aunt Maple. "Hand in hand! You will have to buy me some more vermilion."

But I'm *here*, thought Betony. I must remember that I'm *here*.

She was still on her knees when the shop door was opened cautiously and a tall thin youth came into the shop. He had a narrow, melancholy face, brown unruly hair and spectacles.

He shut the door quickly. "I d-don't want to d-disturb—" he began, and then, "Oh, I thought—"

He looked down at Betony uncertainly.

"D-do you keep scissors?" he asked. "I want to cut some wallpaper and I can only find nail-scissors in the flat. We've not b-been here long and aren't properly unpacked."

Betony got to her feet and found the tin with violets on the lid. The boy selected the largest pair of scissors and paid for them. Then he stood surveying the open cupboard.

"You should have started at the top," he said.

"I was going to," said Betony. "But so many things fell out—"

She could think of nothing more to say but the boy continued to stand by the counter.

He was examining the postcards.

"Alb-bert Terrace," he said. "The west side. Number 26 hasn't changed much, has it? Only the initial in front of D-Dovewood."

"And the front door," said Betony. "We haven't one now."

"What happened to it?" said the boy.

"It was sold, with a bit of the hall," said Betony.

The boy took off his spectacles and looked at her with a bewildered expression.

"B-but I've never heard of a front d-door b-being sold without the house," he said.

"My grandfather sold it," said Betony. "You saw him when you came in the other day." She waited for the boy to go.

But he was still turning over the cards and it struck Betony that he did look very wretched: miserable and very cold.

"You shouldn't have come out without an overcoat," she said.

"The flat's only five minutes away," said the boy. "I d-detest flats b-but it was the only place we could find. I shall have to move out when my father marries again in the spring. Albert Terrace looks like a village street, d-doesn't it?"

"I suppose it does," said Betony.

She hesitated.

"Would you like a cup of tea?"

"Are you going to make one for yourself?" asked the boy.

"Well," said Betony. "Well – not exactly – but—"

"I think I'd b-better b-be getting along," said the boy. "I mean, I've a lot to d-do. B-But thank you very much – I mean – thank you all the same. D-Do you live here with your grandfather? I mean—"

"I live with two old aunts," said Betony. "And I only came here yesterday."

"B-But already you're getting things in order," said the boy. "You seem very much at home."

"I'm not at home anywhere," said Betony. "And I shan't be here for long. I have to go back to the Aunts in the middle of March."

To her consternation she realised that she was on the verge of tears.

"My name's Jacob," said the boy hurriedly. "I'm a student at Chelsea. I'm sorry if I've – I mean I hope you'll soon—"

He turned. The shop bell clanged fiercely as he vanished into the fog.

"I'm a fool," thought Betony. "I should simply have made some tea."

She closed her eyes. Aunt May, majestic in her ancient hat and woollen bedsocks, would be drinking her early-afternoon cup of tea and preserving the Fire of Life with chocolate biscuits. Betony seemed to hear her calling, "Betony! Betony! I can feel a draught. Kindly shut your door and see the doors are shut downstairs."

The lower shelves of the cupboard occupied Betony for the next hour.

6

The China Cottage

The three top shelves were roofed with thick brown paper. Betony climbed the steps and carefully swept off the dust. Then she lifted the paper from the top shelf.

The Dovewoods had lived at Number 26 for generations and the shelf was closely packed with things that had accumulated through the years – things that had outlived their usefulness, things that were broken but might still be repaired, things that were family relics and could not be thrown away.

There was a miscellaneous collection of recipe books, worn luggage straps and keys; there were several broken clocks; there was a Victorian workbox and a long Edwardian sunshade. And there was the china cottage.

As Betony lifted the cottage she discovered that her hands were shaking. Curzon peered down from the top of the cupboard, hissed softly and withdrew.

The cottage was about five inches high, and was white and finely glazed. An outside chimney buttressed one end of it and another chimney thrust up through the painted thatch. The walls were half covered with miniature roses and morning glories.

The cottage stood on a separate plinth, that was moulded into a moss-green hillock, and gilded steps led up to the door.

But all the fairy-tale prettiness was marred by a crack, like a dark flash of lightening, that zigzagged down through the flowers on the front wall.

The crack horrified Betony, and was yet strangely familiar.

She heard Spurrey move on the far side of the cupboard.

"They're only things," he said. "Nothing but things. You needn't pay any attention to them."

"Yes," said Betony. "Yes. But I remember this china cottage. And I remember the crack."

"The cottage has been in the cupboard since I was a boy," said Spurrey. "It was there when your grandmother packed the top shelves."

"Then I can't have seen it," said Betony.

"Don't put it back," said Spurrey. "Linny and Gerard may like to look at it. And Mrs O'Connor will certainly admire the flowers."

Betony climbed down with the cottage and edged round the wardrobe. Spurrey was painting by the light of a blue electric bulb.

"Have you ever thought," he said, "that snow is the wind made visible?"

"No," said Betony. "I never have."

"Last winter," said Spurrey, "I watched the flakes driving down diagonally from the north. And suddenly a few flakes were caught in a cross current of air and flew back against the wind. I saw it happen. But one can't paint it – the wind against the wind."

"I suppose not," said Betony. "Here's the cottage. It must be pretty old."

"Probably late Georgian," said Spurrey. "I don't know how the family acquired it. A pity it's cracked."

He lifted the cottage off its plinth. "Pastilles were burned under the chimneys," he said, "to sweeten the air."

"Perhaps I can find some pastilles," said Betony.

"I've no idea what they were like," said Spurrey.

"They were little cones," said Betony. "But I don't know how I know. D'you think Mrs O'Connor would like to look at the recipe books?"

"Mrs O'Connor never looks at any recipe books," said Spurrey. "She's told me so herself. She cooks by instinct and is guided solely by her culinary impulses. Mrs O'Connor is a great respecter of impulses, especially her own. She took charge of me – on impulse, and may one day vanish – on impulse. But she has a heart of gold."

"Yes," said Betony. "She seemed—"

"Brisk, sensible and shrewd," said Spurrey. "And so she is. But she's also unpredictable. She acts on her impulses and then discovers her reasons. We are none of us as simple as we seem. But leave the recipe books out. They may amuse Linny. She likes to try her hand at puddings when Mrs O'Connor takes a day off."

"The buses have stopped," said Linny. "And we had to walk home. I said to Gerard, 'Isn't it fantastic that Christmas is coming?' and Gerard said, 'It usually does if you wait long enough,' and I said, 'We ought to do something special tonight because Betony's here,' and Gerard said—"

She stopped, staring at the china cottage on the counter. "Oh, what a sweet little house! Oh, isn't it marvellous! Where did it come from?"

"I found it in the cupboard," said Betony. "And Spurrey thought you might be interested in these recipe books."

"And what are these three peculiar little things?" said Linny.

"I think they're the pastilles for burning in the cottage," said Betony. "They were packed into an old workbox. Tea's ready."

7

Vanilla

The shop was closed and Spurrey had settled into his armchair, with Curzon on his knee. The curtains were drawn against the fog which had penetrated into the area. Albert Terrace was totally silent.

"I wanted to do something special," said Linny. "So let's light a pastille in the little house and see what will happen."

"Nothing will happen," said Gerard. "The pastilles are much too old."

"But we could try," said Linny. "I'd like to smell a beautiful smell. What sort of smells were they, Spurrey?"

"I'm afraid I've no experience of them," said Spurrey. "But I believe the most popular scents were orange-flower, rose and vanilla. Light a pastille if you like but I think Gerard may be right."

"I usually am," said Gerard.

"I'd better work a bit of magic then," said Linny. "If I can stroke Curzon seven times before the clock strikes half past six – one, two, three, four, five, six – it's just going to strike – seven. I've done it."

She glanced, half apologetically, at Betony.

"I don't *really* believe I can work magic," she said, "But it's nice to pretend I can."

It was Betony who, at last, managed to light one of the little cones in the china cottage. Curzon lifted his head and growled softly. Then he leapt off Spurrey's knee and retreated, spitting, under the table. But nothing else happened.

They waited.

"What did you expect?" said Gerard.

"Look!" cried Linny. "Look!"

Two thin twists of smoke were rising from the cottage chimneys. Curzon howled suddenly, clawed at the door and was gone.

"I believe I can smell something," said Linny. She leaned over the cottage. "Yes, I'm sure I can."

"Pure imagination," said Gerard.

"But I can," said Linny. "It reminds me of cakes. I think it's vanilla. Yes. That's what it is. It's vanilla."

"Pure imagination," said Gerard.

"I can smell it too," said Betony.

"But there's no scent," said Gerard. "If there were I should smell it. There's no scent at all."

Betony stood up. She was very pale.

"It's too sweet," she said. "Too sweet! We must put out the pastille."

She stumbled to the door.

"I can't stay here," she said, "I'm sorry. I'll – I'll come back. But I can't stay here. I have to go – I have to go."

"There's thick fog outside," said Gerard. "You can't—"

But Betony was already on the stairs.

"She'll get lost in the fog," wailed Linny. "She'll fall in the river. She'll get run over."

"All right," said Gerard. "All right. I'll fetch her back."

"Take my torch," said Spurrey.

"Not much good on a night like this," said Gerard.

The bell was still jangling when he reached the shop and switched on all the lights. But Betony had gone.

8

The Other Shop

Betony returned as precipitately as she had left. Linny and Spurrey, conferring anxiously outside the shop door, saw her emerge suddenly into the blurred light under the street lamp. She was white-faced and breathless.

"I got lost," she said, "but I heard someone shouting so I came as quickly as I could."

"I've been shouting for hours and hours," said Linny. "I thought you'd never come back. I've been shouting and shouting."

"For twenty minutes," said Spurrey.

"I'm sorry," said Betony. "I'm very sorry. I don't quite know what happened."

Spurrey shut the door.

"We'll leave the lights on in the shop for Gerard," he said. "He went out to look for you. You need a hot drink, and so does Linny."

Betony leaned over the fire warming her hands. She was still shivering. "There was the fog," she said, "and then the total darkness when all the street lamps must have gone out. And then there was the wind."

"Wind?" said Spurrey.

"I suppose I was bewildered," said Betony. "I know I lost all sense of direction. Then I found myself in an alley with cobbles under my feet. And the fog was like a great brown wall."

There was a clatter on the stairs and Gerard burst into the room. "Has Betony—?" he began, and then, "Oh, *there* you are. Next time you want to rush off into the night do wait until there's a moon. Where on earth have you been?"

"I don't know," said Betony. "I'm terribly sorry." She hesitated. "I – I found the other shop."

Curzon peered round the door, paused and then stalked to the fire. He lifted his head and sniffed several times. Then he leapt on Spurrey's knee.

"What other shop?" said Gerard.

"The other Dovewood shop," said Betony. "I didn't know there was one."

"There isn't," said Gerard.

"But I found it," said Betony. "And the name was painted over it – *Oliver Dovewood. Pastrycook and Confectioner.*"

"Oliver isn't a family name. And there isn't such a shop," said Gerard.

"It's at the corner where the alley joins the main street," said Betony.

"What alley?" said Gerard. "And what street?"

Betony looked at him helplessly.

"I don't know," she said. "But I felt my way along the alley wall and heard the frozen puddles crack under my feet. And people went by me but I couldn't see them in the fog. There was a lamp at the end of the alley. And *there* was the shop." She stopped.

"It looks old but very prosperous," she added.

"And, in spite of the fog, you could read the *Dovewood*?" said Gerard.

"There were candles in the windows," said Betony. "And there was a wedding cake with a little king and queen on top."

"As far as I know there's never been another Dovewood shop here," said Spurrey.

"And no Dovewood would be called Oliver," said Gerard.

"But I couldn't have imagined the shop," said Betony.

"Couldn't you?" said Gerard. "Was there anyone inside the shop?"

"I think so," said Betony, "but the fog was so thick and brown—"

"Brown fog?" said Gerard. "This is a smokeless zone. We don't get brown fogs."

"But the fog smelt of soot," said Betony.

"Now look," said Gerard. "This is all fantastic nonsense. You've been letting your imagination get the better of you."

"It wasn't imagination," said Betony. "I spoke to an old man, who had stopped to look into the window, and I can tell you exactly what he looked like. He was very small and he had a red, wizened face and sharp, twinkling eyes. He was wearing a long coat and a cap pulled down over his ears. And he wore a battered hat on top of the cap. He had a long staff and a lantern, and there was a wooden rattle tucked into his coat between the third and fourth buttons."

"Sounds like one of the old night watchmen," said Spurrey. "I used to have a print of one in the shop window. I can't remember if I ever sold it."

"It's still there," said Gerard.

"I began to ask the old man how to get back to Albert Terrace," said Betony, "but he shook his head and hobbled away."

"And you didn't speak to anyone else?" said Gerard.

"No," said Betony. "There was a woman looking out of the window over the shop but I couldn't attract her attention."

"And then?" said Gerard.

"Then I heard Linny calling," said Betony. "But I don't know how I got back."

"Now look," said Gerard, "I think I know what happened. You're a Dovewood and you have the Dovewood imagination. And it sometimes takes queer forms. You imagined you smelt vanilla and rushed out into the fog. And found a cake shop, because vanilla suggests cakes. Then, naturally enough, you saw your own name over the shop. You must have noticed the print of the night watchman yesterday when you got out of the taxi and looked in the shop window. So, naturally, you saw a night watchman peering into the imagined shop. You're highly strung. And one can see anything in a fog."

"I can't," said Linny. "I can't see anything."

"I'm not talking to you," said Gerard. "I'm merely offering a rational explanation."

"But it wasn't like that," said Betony, desperately.

"People don't hobnob with night watchmen these days," said Gerard. "And can you be absolutely certain—"

"I'm not certain of anything," said Betony and burst into tears.

"The subject is closed," said Spurrey.

9

Twelfth Night

Mrs O'Connor cooked the Christmas dinner and was persuaded to stay and share it. She presented Spurrey with a large tin of mixed biscuits. There were sunflowers on the lid.

"I've been dreaming of our old garden again," she said. "Silly, if you ask me! D'you know what a house agent said to me the other day? 'Madam,' he said, 'people don't need gardens for modern living, they need garages.' 'Speak for yourself!' I said. 'I need every tree and flower I can get. And I need them in a garden.'" She glanced at Spurrey over the Christmas pudding. "One day I'll get my hands on that wilderness of yours," she said.

"Never," said Spurrey. "I like it as it is."

After Christmas Gerard and Linny settled down to write their "thank you" letters. Betony, having none to write, spent most of her time in the shop. Customers came in for calendars, for New Year cards, for diaries. But the regulars came simply to talk to Spurrey and would edge round the great wardrobe without the smallest pretence that they wanted to buy anything. Betony got to know them. There was the librarian, who played the flute, the schoolmistress who kept white mice because her flat was too small for an Alsatian, the railway porter who collected stamps, and a rosy-cheeked old lady who insisted that she was descended from Cleopatra. There were also the art students, eager, voluble and dogmatic, who argued endlessly round Spurrey's oil stove.

To Betony, they were little more than shadows, who appeared and disappeared, between the hours of nine and five thirty.

Only Jacob, lean, hesitant and lonely, seemed real. Jacob wandered into the shop nearly every day. He would prop himself against the counter and say, "Hallo, B-Betony! Are you at home yet?" Betony never answered the question directly. She felt protected and safe behind the counter but her days were curiously dreamlike.

Once she said, "I can't get used to living with people who like each other. It's extraordinary!"

On the evening of January 6th, Betony wrote:

Dear Aunt May,
Thank you for the little calendar, which came this morning. I see you've drawn a circle round March 15th. I've not forgotten that spring-cleaning must always start on the 16th.
With all good wishes for the New Year, Betony

Betony hesitated before she addressed the envelope. The note was perhaps, too abrupt. She added a postscript.

P.S. This morning Spurrey announced a Giving-Away Day. This can happen at any time. There was only one thing I wanted, a little china cottage that I'd found in the cupboard. Linny begged me to choose something else, but Gerard insisted that I ought to have it, and the old pastilles that can be burnt in it to sweeten the air. So now its mine – a harmless, pretty little ornament as Gerard calls it. B.

Betony addressed and stamped the envelope. Then she took a fresh sheet of notepaper.

Dear Aunt Maple, she wrote. *Thank you for the little calendar. Aunt May sent me one too. I notice you've marked March 15th. Gerard and Linny have gone to the cinema and won't be back till past eight. Spurrey is painting. I shall keep Aunt May's calendar on my mantelpiece and yours in my cloak pocket. I'm sorry the new housekeeper has been impertinent and the gardener has been coming late. I'm sure the milkman didn't mean to be rude. With every good wish for the New Year. Betony.*

Betony addressed and stamped the second envelope. Then she ran upstairs for her cloak. There was still time to catch the last post.

The china cottage stood on the bedside table. It was now surrounded by a miniature hedge of twisted tinsel. Pink and silver Christmas tree balls encircled the tinsel. There was a note propped against the lamp.

> *Gerard said I had to take away the decorations today. But this is magic, so the cottage won't be dangerus. Lots of love, Linny.*

Betony stood staring down at the cottage.

"A harmless, pretty little ornament," she said. "I suppose Gerard's right. But I wish I knew—"

She put on her cloak and walked to the door. Then she hesitated and came back. "A harmless, pretty little ornament!"

Within its tinsel hedge the china cottage shone innocently under the lamp.

Betony had, suddenly, an overwhelming wish to see the smoke rising again from the small gilded chimneys. She took the cottage off the plinth and looked hesitantly at the pastilles. Only two. She took them up in her hand. Then, swiftly, she set one on the plinth and lit it. She waited.

Very slowly, a thread of smoke rose and spiralled above

the cottage roof. In the draught from the door it drifted over Linny's hedge.

There was a faint scent of vanilla.

Betony was still watching the smoke when the room began to darken. At first she was scarcely aware of the change. But the darkness increased. It blurred the outlines of the bed and the chest of drawers, of the bedside table and the lamp itself. For a few seconds the china cottage seemed to shine with its own light. Then it, too, vanished.

The scent of vanilla had grown stronger. Betony stood still. Her hands were cold and she could feel the beating of her heart. She waited.

Then the wind came.

Suddenly it seemed to Betony that the ground was gone from under her feet and she was swept up, weightless and unresisting, into the dark air. She could see nothing and feel nothing. She was carried away in the black gale. And the sound of the wind deafened her.

Rowan

Oliver Dovewood

Time had ceased to have any meaning when the gale subsided and Betony was aware of light, a wavering, remote gleam, that brightened as the wind sank away. She heard distant voices that were faint as echoes. The light increased. Then Betony saw that coloured shadows, like upright reflections in water, were floating round her. She could not see them clearly but she could feel cobbles under her feet.

The light was diffused. It streamed from two curved, candlelit windows and the open door between them. And Betony, looking up, saw the five words that she had expected to see: *Oliver Dovewood Pastrycook and Confectioner.*

Faces pressed round her but they were faces out of

focus, that sharpened and then dissolved like faces seen at the edge of sleep. There was constant pushing but Betony felt nothing of the movement and thrust of the crowd. And the voices remained like thin echoes.

Suddenly, however, there was an explosion of noise – of quick hammer blows and shouts of indignation. And Betony became aware that the insubstantial, shifting figures were eager individuals who were edging their way towards the door of Oliver Dovewood's shop.

Somebody bawled, "Rascals! They have nailed my coat to the window frame," and a woman cried, "I am pinned to you, Sir, by my pelisse. I dare not move, Sir! I dare not move."

"The boys are up to their Twelfth Night tricks again," said a man behind Betony, and another answered, "It is always the same in the City, Sir. Indeed, I marvel that any of us dare congregate outside a confectioner's window on this night of the year. We jeopardise our coat-tails, Sir. We jeopardise them."

"Yet the windows are as good as a show," said the first voice. "And our children would never forgive us if we did not bring them home a Twelfth Night cake."

"True, Sir, true," said the other.

Betony shivered in her red cloak. The crowd was alien and strange, and she was afraid. A stout woman, with ostrich plumes in her bonnet, was forcing her way forward, without waiting for the footman who accompanied her, and Betony was propelled against the nearest window. It was, indeed, as good as a show. It not only glittered with candlelight but was garlanded with artificial flowers and arranged with fantastic iced cakes. Betony had never seen such confectionery. Here was a sugar castle, complete with battlements, turrets and miniature sugar knights, here was a temple with an elegant sugar goddess; here was a Gothic church, a windmill and a rustic cottage surrounded by sugar sheep.

I must tell Linny about them, thought Betony. I must try to remember—" But the people were pressing fiercely towards the door and carried her with them.

Somewhere at the edge of the crowd a hoarse, authoritative voice began to shout. "Make way! Make way! You boys stand aside!" And a child cried, "Here's the constable!"

"Clear away from the door! Let the customers go in! Let the cakes come out!" bellowed the constable.

The crowd shuffled and swayed in the candlelight and there was a brief silence.

The noise began again as several boys were driven out of the door in a struggling group, one protesting violently that he only wanted to buy a cake.

"Then go in at the alley door," cried the woman who had chased them out. "And don't you dare come back among the gentry."

"Be off with you," thundered the constable. "Make way for the cakes!"

Then a new voice broke through the general hubbub and a huge, middle-aged man charged out of the shop. He was without a coat, his shirt sleeves were rolled up and he wore a long white apron. Perched on the back of his head was a wrinkled white cap.

Betony saw him clearly as he plunged down the steps. He was a giant of a man. His heavy features were lightened by an expression of infinite good humour and he had the formidable Dovewood chin.

"Where's that boy?" he roared. "Where's that boy?" And from all sides answering shouts arose.

"Has he been thieving, Mr Dovewood?"

"He cannot be gone far."

"He deserves to be hanged."

"There's been no thieving," roared Oliver Dovewood.

"My shop woman was over zealous. I do not turn away customers. Now where's that boy?"

A small, piping voice came from the corner of the alley. "I'm 'ere, Mr Dovewood. I got me money. A lady give it me when I pick up 'er purse out o' the mud."

Mr Dovewood was already swallowed up by the crowd but Betony heard his great. bellow. "And how much money have you, boy? Sixpence? Then sixpence worth of cake you shall have. I never turn away a customer. Who knows, boy, but one day you may be Lord Mayor of London."

Now most of the crowd was laughing.

Then Oliver Dovewood reappeared on the steps thrusting ahead of him a pale, rough-haired little boy. They vanished into the shop.

"Dovewood is too easy-going and too open-handed," said the woman with the ostrich feathers in her bonnet. "I have always said so. And I have said, too, that he should remove to a more fashionable street."

"Mr Dovewood's customers, Ma'am, come for his cakes. They do not come, Ma'am, to admire the prospect from his shop windows," said a young soldier, whose amiable face was nearly as red as his coat.

The little boy emerged on the steps with a twisted cornucopia of paper in his hands. His friends had apparently edged back to the shop and were waiting for him.

"Mr Dovewood give me enough for all of us!" he cried.

What am I doing here? thought Betony. This is not my time. I must get back to Number 26. She turned and began to push her way towards the edge of the crowd.

She had almost reached the open street when she was jerked to a sudden standstill and, turning quickly, discovered that her cloak had been pinned to the coat of a gentleman who was facing the other way. A little old man dived out of sight as she turned, but Betony had

47

recognised him. He was the old watchman that she had seen on the night of the fog.

"Pray stand still," said the gentleman to whom she was fastened. "There is no need to distress yourself. I will unbutton my coat."

"Yes," said Betony.

"I rode out into the country this morning," said the gentleman, "and on returning paused, for but an instant, to admire my father's illuminations. And, hey presto! I discover that I am attached to a young lady whom I have never seen before. Not that I can see you now—since we are back to back in all this press of people. Have but a little patience, a very little."

He wriggled out of his coat and turned, holding it carefully.

I should not be here, thought Betony. I must not be seen. She pulled the hood of her cloak about her face.

"Now," said the gentleman, "I will endeavour to release us both without damaging either your modesty or my coat. Pray do not move."

He bent down and Betony felt that he was fumbling for the pin.

"I have known," he said, "as many as five or six persons pinned together on Twelfth Night. The boys are very adept at the sport and I have often marvelled at the speed with which the little wretches go about their work. But I myself have never before suffered at their hands. No – but that sounds ungallant! You must forgive me because I am already the prisoner of another young lady – who also wears a red cloak. There! The pin is out. I beg to inform you that you are at liberty. Good evening." He stood up, swept off his hat and turned away.

"Thank you," said Betony. As he turned she had seen by the light of the shop windows that he was young and broad-shouldered and had the Dovewood chin.

II

Mrs Rock

Carriages waited in the ill-lit street and the air smelled of trodden garbage and soot.

I must get back, thought Betony. But she had no idea what to do. *I must get back.*

She looked desperately about her and saw that a woman had come out on the steps of the tall house next to the shop. The woman peered down as Betony looked up.

"Katharine!" cried the woman. "Katharine!" And she flew down the steps and caught Betony in her arms. Betony shivered at her touch.

"So you are come," cried the woman. "Ah, child, I have been near distracted since you wrote that you were sick and could not travel. But I saw a red cloak from the window. And now that you are here, all will be well. Come in! Come in." She hesitated. Then she stepped back with her hands pressed together over her heart. "But you are not Katharine," she said.

"No," said Betony.

"My own wishes deceived me," said the woman and she spoke with sudden violence. "Who are you? You have the look of Katharine – who are you? You are come from the country. Are you come from Katharine? Tell me, tell me."

"I don't know Katharine," said Betony.

"And yet you resemble her," said the woman. "You are a little taller but you are pale and have the same eyes. You would pass for Katharine. Yes, yes! You would pass for her among those who are not too well acquainted with her. You had best come in. We cannot stand here in the street. The mistress is pacing about as usual, lost in her poetical fancies, and may look out of the window. You must come in."

"No," said Betony. "I must go back."

"I implore you to come in," said the woman. "For a short time – a very short time." Her voice was shaking.

"I will take you to my parlour over the shop," she said. "We shall not be disturbed there. I am Mrs Dovewood's housekeeper and am called Mrs Rock. Come in."

"No," said Betony. "This is not my time. I must go back."

"I may, perhaps, be of assistance," said Mrs Rock. "But we cannot converse in the street."

Betony stood irresolute.

"I heard them say *the City* when I was in the crowd," she said. "But I've never been there."

"You are in the City now," said Mrs Rock. "And but a few minutes from Temple Bar. You will scarce reach your home again by lingering in the street. And there are those abroad after dark who are a danger to all honest young women. For your own sake you had best come in."

Betony looked uncertainly at the woman. She was thin and very erect and must once have been handsome. But some anxiety or grief, it seemed, had sharpened her features. She wore a frilled cap and long grey dress, and the keys that hung at her waist jingled softly as she moved.

"I think I've seen you before," said Betony. "You looked out of the window over the shop on the night of the fog."

"I looked out of one of my parlour windows," said Mrs Rock. "Now we must go in."

She had regained her composure and with it, a sort of authority.

She turned and walked up the steps. Betony followed her. There seemed nothing else that she could do.

"This house is somewhat old," said Mrs Rock. "And so, too, is the shop and the bakery under it, which extends beneath the street. The Mistress is for ever refurbishing this house but cares not at all for the rooms above the shop which she and the Master occupied when he was less properous."

Mrs Rock closed the door and picked up a lighted candle that stood on a table by the wall.

"Come," she said and led the way up a curving flight of stairs to a wide landing.

"When the Master purchased this house," she said, "he had an arch made in the wall that he might come and go more freely between the shop and the house. But the Mistress disregards the shop altogether now and would have her genteel acquaintances disregard it too. So the house and the shop are become separate establishments. And the Mistress is become a lady."

"I see," said Betony. "But I must go back."

"The Master himself is contented enough," said Mrs Rock. "And scarce a week goes by but he devises some new confection. As for the Mistress, she has her ambitions, and her carriage."

"I see," said Betony. "But you said you might help me."

Mrs Rock pushed aside a red velvet curtain and Betony followed her on to another landing and through a door on the right into a large firelit room.

There were two great windows, an oval table in the centre of the room and chairs ranged round the walls. There was a long sofa near the fire.

"This is my parlour," said Mrs Rock. "In the old days the Mistress was glad enough to entertain her friends here. But now – what are you staring at, girl?"

"The cottage," said Betony. "The china cottage on the table."

"It was given to me by a poor old Charley," said Mrs Rock.

"Charley?" said Betony.

"A night watchman," said Mrs Rock. "I had occasion to do him a service."

"I can smell vanilla," said Betony.

"I lighted a pastille," said Mrs Rock. "I was in despair because Katharine had written that she could not come."

"I don't understand," said Betony.

"I do not hold with superstitious practices," said Mrs Rock, "but the old Charley had said that if ever I were in need of assistance and wished my wish as the smoke rose—"

Betony walked to the table and picked up the cottage. The white glazed walls were painted with miniature roses and morning glories.

"But this is *my* cottage," cried Betony. "This is mine. But there's no crack."

12

The Old Charley

"How can you lay claim to the cottage when you are but just arrived?" said Mrs Rock. "And why should it be cracked? I intend it for Katharine."

Her voice was harsh.

"I did not understand, at first, why you were here. But now it is clear to me that you are to take Katharine's place until she can come."

"I'm not going to take anyone's place," said Betony. "And neither you nor the old Charley can keep me here. I'm going home."

"But I called – and you came," said Mrs Rock. She hurried on, as though to prevent Betony from protesting further.

"It was on one of the nights when I couldn't sleep. I had come in here from my bedchamber which is next to this room, and I heard the Bucks roaring and hallooing outside. They had run, I suppose, from the taverns of Covent Garden or Jermyn Street. They had with them a poor old Charley, whom they had trussed up and carried off. The Bucks are always at war with the Charleys, and since the Bucks are wild young gentlemen and the Charleys weak and often decrepit they suffer endless pranks at the hands of their tormentors."

"There is no need to tell me this," said Betony. "I'm not going to take Katharine's place."

"There was a bright moon that night," said Mrs Rock, "and I looked out and saw the Bucks rolling the Charley over and over on the cobbles. So I opened the window and shouted that they were a disgrace to the town, as indeed they are. And they waved their hats at me then, and rushed away baying like hounds in full cry. But they left the old Charley behind."

"Will you please listen," said Betony.

"I went down quickly, with my scissors, and cut the ropes that bound him," said Mrs Rock. "And then I helped him up to this room to recover. I mended the fire, gave him a little brandy and laid compresses on his bruises. He was more dead than alive, and he sat here until past four in the morning. Then I went down to the bakehouse, where Mr Dovewood was at work with his men, and the Master himself took the poor old Charley back to his watch-box. And some two months later the old man brought me the china cottage. I have only lighted a pastille once before – to sweeten the air when fog had crept into the house."

Betony put the cottage down on the table. "I'm going back to my grandfather," she said.

"And how will you go?" asked Mrs Rock.

"The crack in the cottage belongs to my time," said Betony. "I shall shut my eyes and think of the crack. And perhaps the wind will come."

"And what of me?" said Mrs Rock.

"I'm sorry but I can't help you," said Betony.

They faced each other across the table with the china cottage between them. In the twinkling radiance of the candle they were isolated in the high shadowy room. Betony shut her eyes. "I'm going back to my own room," she thought. "The cottage is by the bed and the crack is like a flash of lightning – a flash of lightning. I'm going back to Spurrey and Linny and—"

There was a sudden shout and then a violent knock on the door.

"*Mon Dieu!*" cried Mrs Rock. "The Master! Oh, *Mon Dieu! Mon Dieu!*"

As Betony opened her eyes Mrs Rock caught her by the shoulders and thrust her behind the curtains.

There was another loud knock.

"Come in, Sir," cried Mrs Rock.

Oliver Dovewood charged into the room. "I must have reinforcements," he roared. "My customers are advancing on me in battalions, in regiments, in great armies. I have never known such a Twelfth Night."

"I will come down to the shop immediately, Sir," said Mrs Rock.

"No, no!" shouted Oliver Dovewood. "That would never do. Mrs Dovewood would be outraged if her housekeeper were to be seen selling cakes in the shop."

"Then how can I assist you, Sir?" said Mrs Rock. "I cannot send either of the maids because Annie is altering a gown for the Mistress and I gave Clara permission to visit her aunt."

"I understood that our new Betsy was to arrive today," said Oliver Dovewood. "She is not yet known in the neighbourhood and must help in the shop for this one night. I will explain matters to Mrs Dovewood. Where is the girl?"

"She is a little fatigued, Sir," said Mrs Rock quickly. "And, Sir, she is from the country and quite unaccustomed to—"

"No matter! No matter!" shouted Oliver Dovewood. "She shall have charge of the buns. Any simpleton can sell buns. She shall be properly recompensed and shall sleep late tomorrow."

With that he rushed out of the room.

Mrs Rock looked towards the curtains. "You heard the Master's orders?" she said.

Betony emerged. "I could hardly help hearing," she

said. "But, Oliver Dovewood is not my master. And I'm not the girl from the country."

"Yet you wear a red country cloak," said Mrs Rock. "And you came when I called." She put up her hand when Betony would have spoken.

"I have waited and worked through the long years," said Mrs Rock, "sustained by the one hope – that Katharine could be with me again."

"Again?" said Betony.

"I have known her since she was a little child," said Mrs Rock. "She was as solitary as I, and I have watched over her from a distance. But it was necessary that I should work, and the Mistress would never have permitted me to have Katharine here. So I settled her in the country. But now that she is older there are reasons why she must be got away from the village. She is both pretty and innocent and it seems that some gentleman in the neighbourhood has taken note of her. She has written of him, in vague terms, several times. But gentlemen are not for her. She is the child of servants and must remain honestly in her station. Do you understand? No gentleman must be permitted to—"

A boy in a white cap thrust his head round the door and shouted that the Master was growing impatient and that the girl from the country must come down to the shop at once.

Outside on the landing a clock struck sharply and Betony counted the strokes. It was six o'clock.

Spurrey was painting and Linny and Gerard were at the cinema.

Betony saw, with acute distress that Mrs Rock was in tears. The woman wept silently, with a hand pressed to her heart, as though her grief caused intolerable pain.

"Look," said Betony, "I can't take Katharine's place, but I don't mind selling buns for a little while."

13

The Bun Table

The shop was large and overcrowded. It glittered with both lamplight and candlelight.

The great looking glasses on the walls were hung with garlands of artificial flowers and endlessly reflected the shop and the illuminations so that shining vistas of lights and cakes seemed to open on every side. Bouquets decorated the counters, and the show glasses, which held brandy balls and sugar sticks, were festooned with paper roses.

Cakes, of all sizes and designs, were ranged on the long counters but the most fantastic and elaborate cakes were placed apart, on separate salvers.

Here were more castles, towers and abbeys, here were romantic ruins and rustic dwellings. Here were dragons and lions, gods and shepherds, cats, princes and serpents all in delicately-coloured confectionery. In the centre of the shop a mountainous cake stood alone and was crowned by the Temple of Flora. Betony stood staring about her.

Linny would like all this, she thought. I must remember everything about it.

The shop, prolonged by its shining image in every mirror, appeared like some vast, flower-decked hall where an improbable miniature world had been created in confectionery.

Suddenly Betony caught sight of herself in a looking glass on the far wall. She scarcely recognised her own reflection.

She wore the clothes that Mrs Rock had hurriedly brought to her—a long, high-waisted dress, with a frill at the neck, a white apron and a mob cap.

Am I still Betony Dovewood? she thought.

Then Oliver Dovewood came bustling up. "So there you are," he cried. "You must take charge of the buns."

He looked down at her kindly. "You shall sleep late tomorrow," he said. Then he led the way towards the side door which opened on the alley. Near the door a long table was set out with trays of buns and a handsome young woman was dealing briskly with a crowd of shabby customers.

"Now here are the plain halfpenny buns," said Oliver Dovewood. "And here are the plum buns which are a penny each. And here are the frosted plum buns, and they are a penny halfpenny."

"Yes," said Betony, and hastily added, "Sir."

"Many of my fellow confectioners will not trouble to sell buns on Twelfth Night," said Oliver Dovewood, "since cakes are more profitable. But I hold that any honest child, who wishes to spend his penny on a bun, should be treated with that same civility that the great Duke himself would receive should he desire to purchase my Temple of Flora."

"Yes, Sir," said Betony.

The handsome young woman curtsied and hurried away.

"The children know that if they behave in a disorderly manner they will instantly be turned out of the shop," said Oliver Dovewood. "Now, my dear, I leave you with the buns."

So Betony was left with the buns and a crowd of small, pale, down-at-heel creatures who jostled round the table.

Most of the girls were in frayed shawls and broken

bonnets and the boys in patched jackets. Some of the children were barefooted and appeared to wear bundles of rags which hung loosely from their thin shoulders. A few women stood quietly, their hands rolled in their aprons.

Betony served each in turn, watching to see that none of them snatched a bun, and struggling with the unfamiliar money. Once, when she hesitated to accept two tiny coins, the girl who had proffered them said indignantly, "Them's proper fardens, Miss."

Once Betony heard a distant clock strike and once the boy in the white cap brought her fresh supplies. And still her small, eager customers rushed through the side door, pushing, whispering and always struggling to get near the buns. In the main part of the shop the sale of cakes continued and Oliver Dovewood's cheerful bellow greeted all his customers. But Betony concentrated on the buns. Plain buns, plum buns, and frosted plum buns!

Suddenly she found Mr Dovewood beside her. He put a newspaper down on the bun table.

"There is an old Charley," he said, "who is a friend of Mrs Rock's. The poor fellow is a great newspaper reader but cannot well afford to purchase a newspaper for himself. So I see to it that his buns are always wrapped in the day's news."

"Yes, Sir," said Betony.

"You are a good girl," said Oliver Dovewood. "And I should be glad enough to have you in the shop if you were not already attached to Mrs Dovewood's establishment. I have had my eye on you and saw how you made the urchins wait their turns, and how you checked their too-eager fingers. Soon we shall close the shutters and then you shall go to your bed."

The distant clock struck again and he hurried away.

A few minutes later the old night watchman limped through the side door. His red, wizened face wore an expression of child-like innocence but his eyes were sharp and twinkling.

"Why did you pin my cloak—" began Betony.

"Well now," said the old Charley. "Well now, there weren't no harm done."

"But you know I can't stay here," said Betony. "You know this isn't my time."

"I know what I knows. And I sees what I sees," said the old Charley. "And that Mrs Rock she save me from the Bucks."

"I know," said Betony. "But—"

"Them Bucks, they hunts us Charleys and they harries us Charleys," said the old man. "They runs off with our lanterns and overturns our watch-boxes. They trips us up and ties us up and rolls us in the gutter. Their hearts is as hard as their ways is wicked. But they can't take away me powers."

"But I must go back," said Betony.

"I got shadow sight, what they calls second sight," said the old Charley. "So don't you go a-hardening that heart o' yourn. You find a way, Miss Bet, and do what it tell you. And now I wants two halfpenny buns for me supper."

As Betony wrapped the buns she glanced down at the newspaper. It was dated January 6th, 1826.

14

A Note on the Mantelpiece

"I called and called," said Linny. "Where *have* you been?"

"In the City," said Betony. "But I meant to be back before you got home."

"We didn't wait for the second film," said Gerard. "Linny wanted to see that you were still here."

"I came as soon as I could after I heard her calling," said Betony. "I thought of the crack."

"You were in the City and you heard Linny calling!" said Gerard. "And you thought of the crack. What crack?"

"The crack in the cottage," said Betony. "But, please—"

"And why on earth did you go to the City?"

"I was needed," said Betony. "I'm – I'm still rather confused."

"You're not the only one," said Gerard. "Now suppose you tell us—"

"Don't bully the girl," said Spurrey. "Betony isn't a child."

"I'm sorry if you were worried about me," said Betony. "I'm very sorry."

She began to unfasten her cloak.

"They thought I was from the country," she said. "I'm tired – I'm terribly tired. They thought I was a country girl in a red cloak."

"Go to bed," said Spurrey. "Linny will bring you up some supper on a tray."

"Perhaps you could just tell us what you've been doing in the City," said Gerard. "And who it was that thought you were a country girl."

"I've been selling buns," said Betony. "That's all. Selling buns."

Next morning was mild, damp, windless, and pitch dark when Betony tucked her note into an envelope and propped it up on the mantelpiece. Then there was a tentative knock on the door and Linny slipped into the room.

"I thought I smelt vanilla," she said. "Have you—?"

"Yes," said Betony.

"I thought you had," said Linny. "Why have you got your cloak on? It's only half past six."

"I'm going back," said Betony.

"Oh no!" cried Linny. "Oh no!" She stood hesitating, clutching her blue dressing-gown round her.

"You went to the other shop last night, didn't you?" she said. "And now you're going back there. And it's the last pastille."

"Yes," said Betony.

"That's what I thought," said Linny. "But why must you go back? I want you to stay here." Suddenly she flung her arms round Betony. "I like you," she cried. "I like you very much. And we're all comfortable together. So why must you go back? Why?"

"It seems that I'm needed," said Betony. "There's a woman called Mrs Rock and I left her in tears. She tried to hold me but I pushed her away. I can't bear to see people cry. There's a note on the mantelpiece for Spurrey."

"Is Mrs Rock nice?" asked Linny.

"I don't know," said Betony. "She looks as though she's had a miserable life. There's a kind of hardness about her, and she speaks with authority but—"

"My magic hedge didn't work and I hate the cottage," said Linny. "I *hate* it. I wish I could break it into a million pieces."

"There's something you can do for me," said Betony. "If you see Jacob, tell him I shan't be away for long."

"How long?" asked Linny.

"Probably only a few days."

"Of course I can always shout and shout until you come back," said Linny.

"I can come back when I think of the crack," said Betony, "but I shall stay till a girl called Katharine arrives. So you're not to shout."

"Who's Katharine?"

"I don't know," said Betony. "She's coming from the country."

"You look pretty awful," said Linny, "as though you've been awake all night. Shall I just make you a cup of tea?"

"No," said Betony. "Go back to bed."

"What would you do if *I* cried?" said Linny. "If I cried and cried and wouldn't stop? Then you couldn't go away. It's quite easy to cry, and I feel like crying. I think I will."

Betony stooped and kissed her.

"You won't cry," she said, "because there's nothing to cry about. I promise I'll come back."

Linny turned and ran out of the room.

Thin smoke was rising from the gilded chimney and drifting over Linny's hedge. Betony switched off the light.

The cottage seemed to shine, momentarily, with its own small, unearthly radiance. Then it vanished. The scent of vanilla filled the room and Betony was swept up into the dark.

15

The Garret

"So you are returned," said Mrs Rock. "I lighted a pastille but had no hope of seeing you again."

The fire was already burning in her parlour and smoke still rose from the gilded chimneys of the cottage.

"I came because you needed help," said Betony.

"I was in despair," said Mrs Rock. "But now—" her voice became suddenly brisk and authoritative – "now that you are here you will be known as Betsy. Do you understand?"

"But the other girl is called Katharine," said Betony.

"When she arrives she, too, will be called Betsy," said Mrs Rock. "Servants come and go and it would distract the Mistress if she were forced to recollect a number of different names. So our housemaids are permitted but three names – Anne, Betsy or Clara."

"I see," said Betony.

"I shall not ask your true name," said Mrs Rock. "It is best that I should not know it. And I shall not ask where you are come from. It is sufficient that you are here."

"Yes," said Betony.

"You will address me as 'Ma'am' when you answer me," said Mrs Rock sharply. "And you will remember your curtsy. Your household duties will not be difficult and I require but three things of the maids – honesty, health and clean hands."

"Yes," said Betony, and added "Ma'am."

"I see that you have brought nothing with you," said

Mrs Rock. "So my own old box must serve for yours. Fortunately I prepared it for Katharine. Clara will doubtless wish to inspect your possessions. She must never suspect that you are not Katharine."

"But surely when the real Katharine comes—" began Betony.

"When Katharine comes I shall, myself, deal with any difficulties that may arise," said Mrs Rock. "You will meet all the servants at the Reading."

"The Reading?" said Betony.

"In many households the Scriptures are read each morning," said Mrs Rock. "But the Mistress believes that poetical writings are equally beneficial and can edify and uplift all those who hear them. So she reads her own works to us – usually those stanzas that she has produced the day before. Apart from the Readings the Mistress has little to do with the servants, who are in my charge. Annie, however, often acts as Mrs Dovewood's lady's maid."

"I see – Ma'am," said Betony.

"The present Mrs Dovewood is the master's second wife," said Mrs Rock. "She was herself a Dovewood, belonging to some distant branch of the family. The Master, I believe, married her in the belief that she would prove a tender parent and friend to his young son, Mr Alexander, who was then four years old. But unfortunately—"

She stopped.

"The Mistress has always been much taken up with her literary work," she said. "Her genteel friends declare that she is a genius."

"And is she?" asked Betony.

"I have no means of telling," said Mrs Rock. "I know nothing of poetry. "But the Mistress is excessively ambitious – both for herself and for Mr Alexander."

"Now I had best show you where you are to sleep. You will have the small garret to yourself. It is over Mr Alexander's study, where he works in the daytime."

"Yes, Ma'am," said Betony.

The garret had bare floor boards and a low window. There was a bed against the wall, a wooden chair and a stand that held a jug, basin and candlestick. A text, badly executed in curling red letters, hung over the bed. *Servants, be obedient to them that are your masters. Eph. 6:5.*

"That is Annie's work," said Mrs Rock.

"If you don't mind I'll take it down," said Betony.

"You will do no such thing," said Mrs Rock. "Annie will wake you in the mornings. She is an early riser and obliges me by carrying out the unwelcome task which I used to relegate to each maid in turn. She will expect to see the text on the wall if she has to shake you awake."

"I hope that won't be necessary," said Betony.

"Your cloak may hang on the door and your present clothes had best be hid under the mattress," said Mrs Rock. "I should perhaps warn you that since Annie has the ear of the Mistress and is besides, over-careful of her conscience, you should not speak too freely before her. Do you understand me?"

"Yes," said Betony.

"With Clara you will scarcely need to open your mouth," said Mrs Rock, "since she chatters away all day."

"Yes," said Betony.

"The Mistress insists that her household must be regulated and ordered as in the most aristocratic families," said Mrs Rock. "And I strive to satisfy her with the small body of domestics at my command. But my task is not easy. So my authority must never be questioned. Do you understand me?"

"Yes," said Betony.

Mrs Rock lit the candle on the stand from the one she carried. "You will have quiet here," she said. "The cook, Annie, and Clara sleep in the garrets on the other side. You must not think that I lack gratitude. Now I will fetch the gown and cap that you wore last night."

Betony sat down on the bed. It creaked and rustled and she discovered that the mattress was stuffed with straw. It was clear that Mrs Dovewood's domestics were not pampered. What am I doing here? thought Betony. What am I doing here? She wondered if Linny had gone back to bed.

Smoke drifted past the window and she got up and looked out. It was still half dark but she could see, below, grass and a bare tree, surrounded by high walls. The right-hand wall flanked the alley down which she had stumbled on the night of the fog. Beyond the end wall there appeared to be stables and a coach house opening on a mews. All round towered dimly-lighted houses with smoking chimneys. Noise rose from the unseen streets: the rumble of waggons, the cries of street vendors, and the distant wailing of a child.

Then Mrs Rock returned with the clothes.

"Come to my parlour when you are dressed," she said. "Now make haste. You have no time to look out of the window."

"Yes – Ma'am." said Betony.

May   or Hawthorn

16

The Reading

"It is time for the Reading," said Mrs Rock, and Betony followed her through the curtained arch. A bell rang as they reached the hall.

"The Mistress is in the library," said Mrs Rock. "You will stand between Annie and Clara. And do not forget your curtsy."

The other servants were crowding up from the basement: two girls, a footman, a man and a boy. Mrs Rock hurried to their head. Betony stood hesitating, until a rosy-cheeked girl pulled her into the line. Mrs Rock tapped on a closed door, and a deep voice cried, "Enter."

The library was at the back of the house, and, through two tall windows, Betony glimpsed the bare tree and the grass. An imposing arch led from the library into a large front parlour, which overlooked the street. But Mrs

Dovewood was so arresting a figure that Betony hardly noticed her surroundings.

Mrs Dovewood sat, facing the arch, at a lamplit table. And she was so like Aunt May that Betony caught her breath.

The Mistress was a large woman, with heavily rouged cheeks and the Dovewood chin. Her sandy hair was bunched, in curls, on her temples and she wore an ornate morning cap and a yellow cashmere shawl. She appeared to be lost in a poetical reverie and did not look up when each of the maids curtsied and wished her "Good morning". The table was scattered with quill pens, several ink-stands and innumerable sheets of paper.

The servants, led by Mrs Rock, formed a semi-circle in front of the arch between the two rooms.

They waited.

Mrs Dovewood picked up a pen, crossed out a single word and, at last, looked directly at Mrs Rock.

"Are all the servants present?" she asked.

"Yes, Madam," said Mrs Rock.

"I observe that we have a new Betsy."

"Yes, Madam," said Mrs Rock.

"I trust that she is healthy," said the Mistress. "The last Betsy coughed, on several occasions, during the Readings. And you know that I cannot endure the smallest sign of ill health. I would have all my domestics in perfect health."

"Yes, Madam," said Mrs Rock.

Mrs Dovewood began to collect her scattered papers. "Where is the Master?" she asked. "And where is Mr Alexander?"

"The Master has, perhaps, forgot the time, Madam," said Mrs Rock. "And, since the morning is so mild, Mr Alexander may be preparing to ride out into the country again."

"Let them be fetched," said Mrs Dovewood. The boy was sent running to the bakehouse while Mrs Rock herself went to look for Alexander. Five minutes later Oliver Dovewood appeared with Alexander behind him. The Master had removed his apron and put on his coat but still wore his white cap on the back of his head. Alexander was in riding boots and carried his hat under his arm. Betony recognised him at once as the young man to whom she had been pinned on Twelfth Night.

"Your cap, Mr Dovewood!" cried the Mistress and Oliver Dovewood snatched it off and thrust it into his pocket. Then Alexander and he sat down at the table and Mrs Rock and the boy slipped back into their places.

"Proceed, my dear Mrs Dovewood. Proceed!" said Oliver Dovewood.

The Mistress shifted her papers and began to read. Her heroine, it appeared was searching for her husband who had set off on some obscure venture, and had never returned. The poor lady had now reached Arabia but seemed to be faring no better than before despite her exotic surroundings.

The poem was incredibly romantic and bad. Yet only Alexander showed obvious uneasiness and turned such a steady scrutiny on the tree outside the window that Betony guessed he had retreated into his own thoughts. She, herself, began unobtrusively to study her fellow servants.

Next to Mrs Rock stood the cook, a red-faced dumpling of a creature whose fat hands were clasped on her apron.

Then came an ungainly young woman with a moon-face and small pursed mouth. Her hands hung at her sides and she looked as though she had never smiled in her life. Her appearance of passive humility was belied, however, by her eyes which were sharp and closely set. This could only be Annie of the over-careful conscience.

As Betony glanced at her their eyes met for an instant and Betony was startled by the woman's curious, cat-like stare, and her expression of malignant disapproval.

The girl who had pulled her into the line, would then be Clara. She stood on Betony's other side and was as rosy and neat as a pretty doll. She wore a pink ribbon in her cap and her eyes were fixed steadily on Mrs Dovewood.

The footman was a tall youth in a green livery, the man was thin and stooping and the boy had the face of a lively cherub marred only by a black eye. Betony supposed that he had been fighting.

The Reading was drawing to a close. Suddenly Mrs Dovewood thrust her papers aside and rose to her feet. She flung back her head and clasped her hands as she delivered her final lines.

> *The marble garden house was set*
> *About with rose and violet,*
> *And herbs, like tamarisk and musk*
> *Perfumed, with scent, the Arabian dusk.*
> *The lady viewed the distant grove*
> *In hopes to see her absent love*
> *But he, to his eternal shame,*
> *Thought not of her, nor ever came.*

"*Nor ever came*," repeated Mrs Dovewood. Alexander picked up his hat and murmured a few words.

"I beg, Alexander, that you will speak loud enough for me to hear," said Mrs Dovewood.

"A tamarisk, Madam, is not an herb," said Alexander.

"Then what, pray, is it?" demanded the Mistress.

"It is an evergreen shrub, Madam," said Alexander.

"True genius has no need to concern itself with those petty details that are found only in botanical publications," said Mrs Dovewood. "Is it not time that you set off for the country?"

"Indeed it is, Madam," said Alexander. "I thank you, Madam, for reminding me."

On Betony's right there was a sudden stir. Mrs Rock had covered her face with her hands and was sobbing quietly.

There was consternation among the servants.

"There, Ma'am, there!" cried Clara. "Don't take on so, Ma'am. I'll help you up to your parlour, Ma'am. It's only potery, Ma'am, but the Mistress do write so beautiful it's no wonder as you're affected. I'll make you some tea, Ma'am. Oh, don't take on so! There, Ma'am, there!"

Alexander opened the door for them and followed them out into the hall.

"I had no wish to agitate the sensibilities of any of my domestics," said Mrs Dovewood. But she was smiling.

17

Clara

Betony stood alone in the hall.

Annie had followed Mrs Dovewood into the front parlour and the other servants had vanished into the basement. Oliver Dovewood had returned to the bake-house.

As Betony hesitated at the foot of the stairs Clara came flying down.

"So you're our new Bet!" she cried. "Well now, Mrs Rock say as you're to help me with the beds. I don't know what come over poor Mrs Rock. I never seen her like that before. I'd have made her some tea but she say No. You got your box open yet, Bet?"

"Not yet," said Betony.

"You got a dream book, Bet?"

Betony shook her head.

"I lost my dream book," said Clara. "Or maybe that Annie have took it. She don't hold with dreams. But, d'you know Bet, last night I dream of a sojer, him as I seen in the street. You ever dream of a sojer, Bet?"

"No," said Betony.

The door of the front parlour opened softly and Annie appeared. She looked at Clara disapprovingly.

"So there you are, Clara, wasting the Mistress' time with the new Betsy," she said. "The Mistress pays you for your time, Clara, and it all belongs to her – every minute of it. You never see your duty clear, Clara."

"And you sees your duty so clear, Annie, as you don't see nothing else," said Clara. "This is our new Betsy."

"I do as my conscience bids me," said Annie. "And *that* I shall continue to do."

The clock on Mrs Rock's landing struck suddenly.

"Here are you chattering and gossiping, and another hower's gone," said Annie.

> *"Death is nearer,*
> *Heaven is dearer,*
> *Let me see my duty clearer."*

She turned to Betony. "I don't know why you're here," she said. "But you give me the creeps. If any was to tell me you were up to no good I'd not gainsay them. You give me the real creeps. Now I have to trim that bonnet for the Mistress. But you'll not be here long, Betsy. I can tell you that. You'll not be here long."

"You got the manners of a nasty toad, Annie," said Clara as Annie slipped back into the front parlour.

What am I doing here? thought Betony. Why did I come?

"The beds is waiting, Bet," said Clara. "We has to turn the mattresses every day and switch the bedding and shake the bed curtains. I seen that sojer when I were cleaning me front windows. And he smile at me, Bet. Honest he did." And she began to sing.

> *"Why, sojers, why*
> *Should we be melancholy, boys?*
> *Why, sojers, why?*
> *Whose business 'tis to die?*

But I wouldn't want me sojer's head to be swep' off by a nasty cannon ball," said Clara. "You got any song books, Bet?"

They made the beds. They emptied the washbasins. They swept and dusted and polished. And Clara never stopped talking and singing except to run to the window to see who was passing in the street or coming down the alley.

"That Annie don't approve o' singing," said Clara. "And she speak to the Missus if she hear or see any bit o' wickedness. So don't let Annie catch you curling your hair, Bet, or talking to a sojer. No followers is allowed here." She laughed.

"But we has 'em, just the same," she said. "We has 'em."

Mrs Rock appeared briefly and inspected the bedrooms. She was perfectly composed. Betony's box, she said, had been carried up to the garret.

"And you had best open it and shake out your gowns," she said. "You may have fifteen minutes off from work."

"Thank you, Ma'am," said Betony, and remembered to curtsy.

Betony found a large, wooden box standing near the bed. The key turned easily and she thrust back the lid. Inside the box were dresses and aprons, frilled caps, underclothes and neatly rolled stockings, both black and white. There were two pairs of cloth shoes and one pair of leather, with very thick soles.

Under the clothes were two old penny songbooks, a cheap hand-mirror, a pincushion, a piece of soap and a comb. A few other oddments were wrapped in a worn black worsted petticoat at the bottom of the box.

Betony left out the mirror, the soap and the comb. She shook out the clothes and returned them to the box.

Then she sat down on the bed. The dream-like winter morning seemed interminable and she felt curiously light-headed. She wondered vaguely if Jacob had paid his usual visit to the shop. Then steps clattered on the stairs and she heard Clara's voice.

" 'Tis but in vain
I mean not to upbraid you, boys,
'Tis but in vain
For sojers to complain—"

Clara peered round the door.

"Mrs Rock say as I'm to tell you, Bet, to dust Mr Alexander's study," she said. "We dursn't scarce touch it when he's at home. It's so full o' bits o' weeds you'd think you was in the middle o' some raggedy field. And what he wants with all that green stuff and pieces o' trees we can't none of us hazard a guess. He keeps hisself to hisself, do Mr Alexander."

"Does he?" said Betony.

"Annie say as the Missus intends him to marry a young country lady, as'll make him a rich, genteel wife," said Clara. "And the Master's to buy him a nice bit o' land, so he'll be a proper gentleman. That's what the Missus intends and that's how it'll be. Now don't you go a-moving Mr Alexander's buckets. The study's under this garret, Bet, and I'm off to clean me windows. Here's yar broom and dustpan, and a duster."

"Well, I hope you'll see your soldier," said Betony.

"You got a kind heart, Bet," said Clara. "You not said two words all the morning but you got a kind heart."

76

18

The French Footman

Alexander's study was a bare work-room. The floor was uncarpeted and the two tall windows uncurtained. There was a table under one of the windows, and several shelves of books.

The "bits o' weeds" were everywhere. There were buckets of twigs, saucers of moss, berries and dried seedpods. On the table was a simple press made of two pieces of board weighted with bricks. Betony began to sweep the floor, lifting each bucket and setting it down in the same place. She worked slowly. Without Clara's chatter and sudden bursts of song her thoughts wandered and, more and more often, she was forced to lean on her broom. She was aware that she was very cold. Then suddenly, darkness edged her vision. Her last conscious thought was: I believe I'm going to faint.

"*Mon Dieu!*" said Mrs Rock. "*Mon Dieu!* Your first day here and you must swoon on Mr Alexander's floor. If the Mistress hears of this I shall be told to send you packing. Can you stand if I assist you?"

"I think so," said Betony. "I don't usually behave like this. I suppose it's because I've had nothing to eat this morning."

"It is fortunate that I came up here to see that nothing was displaced," said Mrs Rock. She helped Betony to her feet.

"You shall rest on my sofa until you are fully recovered," she said. "You should have told me that you have had no breakfast."

Betony lay back on the sofa.

"The other servants must not guess what has occurred," said Mrs Rock. "*Mon Dieu!* I would not, for all the world, have Annie know. Remain here and I will fetch you something from the kitchen."

"Why do you say *Mon Dieu?*" asked Betony.

"I had a – a friend who was a Frenchman," said Mrs Rock. "His parents had escaped with him, during the Revolution. He was a boy then. After they died he became a footman in the house where I was a housemaid. Now, you are not to stir."

The door closed and Betony heard the key turn in the lock.

I could still go back, thought Betony. Linny would be pleased.

The china cottage had been moved to the mantelpiece. Down below in the street, carts rattled over the cobbles and there was constant shouting. A man went by crying, "Any ole' clo'? Any ole' clo'?"

Betony shut her eyes.

I'm leading a double life, she thought. But I could still go back.

Mrs Rock returned with a tray and carried it to the sofa. Then she sat down in the armchair on the other side of the hearth.

"Now listen to me," she said.

"I think I've listened enough," said Betony.

She looked across at Mrs Rock.

"You know Mrs Dovewood's poetry isn't worth crying over," she said. "It's awful stuff."

"I wept," said Mrs Rock, "because the poor, patient lady in the poem still watched for her husband. And I no longer watch for mine – since he will not return. I know that now. I have known it for years."

"The French footman?" said Betony.

"Yes," said Mrs Rock.

She leaned forward, staring at the fire.

"I never had eyes for any other man. He was as solitary as I. *I* could never mix easily with the other servants, and *he* was a foreigner. We were married when I was eighteen. He was always a foreigner to the other servants – but he was my husband. So I was no longer alone."

"I see," said Betony.

"In 1814 the strange peace overtook us all," said Mrs Rock. "Boney was no longer cock o' the walk and the allies were in Paris. And Henri said he must return to France to discover what was become of his relatives. He would have been reckoned a gentleman if he had stayed in France."

"I see," said Betony.

"But I would not go with him," said Mrs Rock. "We had saved money enough – but I would not go."

"But why?" said Betony.

"I had married a footman and *not* a gentleman," said Mrs Rock. "And so I told Henri. And I had no wish to be despised by his genteel French relations. I had no knowledge of French ways and but a few words of the French tongue. In short, I would not go. And so I told him, over and over again. But Henri persisted. He said that he was married to me and not to my station. He said that the footman and the French gentleman were the same man, and that I was that man's wife. And I replied that a man's position in the world was what the world judged him by. I have seen that often enough. And I said that I was a servant and did not hold with servants who sought to rise above their proper stations. I have always held that opinion – and nothing will shake it.

"For three weeks we quarrelled – when we were free of our household duties. But I had the last word. The child was still very young and my mother, in the village, cared for her. I said that I could not leave her."

"Katharine?" said Betony.

Mrs Rock was silent.

"Henri sailed from Brighton," she said at last. "I had several letters from him saying that there had been great destruction and that family affairs would keep him in France. He begged me to join him, with the child. But I always wrote that he should return to us. Perhaps his pride was greater than mine. I think, now, that he is dead. After the war with Boney broke out again there were no more letters."

"And Katharine?" said Betony.

"She knows nothing," said Mrs Rock.

"But why not?" said Betony. "Why not?"

"Because I had to plan for us both," said Mrs Rock. "After Henri was gone I could not bear to continue in the house where we had been together, so I brought Katharine to a village nearer to London and boarded her with an honest simple family. And there she has remained. She has her father's eyes and dark hair and is considered handsome. As for me, after leaving several situations in London I became Mrs Dovewood's housekeeper. But the Mistress does not know that I have been married and have a daughter. The Mistress expects her servants to have only Dovewood interests at heart."

"I see," said Betony.

"When Katharine was older," said Mrs Rock, "I told her that she was an orphan and that I had been a close friend of her mother's. And this she accepted without question."

"But," began Betony.

"There was but one way in which Katharine and I could be together under this roof," said Mrs Rock. "Katharine would have to be took on as a servant here.

That is what I planned years ago and that is the hope that alone has sustained me."

"But I don't see why Katharine mustn't know that you're her mother," said Betony.

"Because she is innocent and gentle, and could never sustain the burden of duplicity that would be necessary if we were to remain here," said Mrs Rock. "I, myself, am strong enough to keep my natural tenderness and concern for her in check. Indeed, I have never dared to show her—"

"I see," said Betony.

"There are servants, now, walking the London streets because they have no work," said Mrs Rock. "But here I have security and a sort of home. I shall not be able to lavish on Katharine all that fondness and partiality that I could wish, but I shall instruct and guard her. In the village where she now is, she is exposed to dangers of which she has little knowledge. I told you that some neighbouring gentleman had sought her acquaintance."

"Yes," said Betony.

"I would not have Katharine suffer as I have suffered," said Mrs Rock. "One should remain in one's proper station. Every good servant hopes for advancement and that I have achieved. But I am still a servant. And I respect my calling."

She spoke with sudden violence.

"Katharine must study to do likewise."

"Things have changed a lot," said Betony.

But Mrs Rock seemed not to hear.

"I have told no other living soul what I have told you," she said. "Now you must give me your absolute promise never to speak of what you know."

"Very well," said Betony.

"I have your word?"

"Yes," said Betony. "But has Katharine herself ever been asked if she wants to come here?"

"Katharine will come because I have planned and contrived to have her come," said Mrs Rock. "She will do as she is bid."

There was a sudden shout in the street below. "Hey there, Miss! You've dropped your cloth down into the area. Can you catch it, Miss, if I throw it from the steps?"

There was a brief pause and then they heard Clara's voice, gay, laughing and apologetic.

"Thank you, sojer. Oh dear! Now I've dropped me duster. Oh thank you, sojer!"

19

The Servant's World

Katharine did not come. And if Mrs Rock had any news she kept that news to herself. She watched the running of the house with seeming composure but Betony was aware of the housekeeper's growing anxiety. She gave Betony no chance, though, to speak to her alone.

Betony herself felt that she was caught in some curious, interminable dream. Sometimes she stood still and seemed to hear Linny's voice: "I wish Betony would come home. Why doesn't she come?"

Sometimes it was Jacob who asked, "Is B-Betony b-back yet? Surely it's time she came b-back."

She longed for the shop, and for Spurrey's wandering dissertations on painting and history. She was homesick for Number 26.

When she remembered Dovewood House and the two Aunts she thrust the thoughts aside.

The servants' world, that existed below stairs, had its own fixed hierarchy and laws, and its own rivalries. Clara carried on a perpetual war with the footman; the cook alternately spoiled and bullied the boy, and Annie was regarded as a model of virtue, a source of information and a plague. She was also feared.

When Mrs Rock retreated from the table to her parlour, Clara's dreams were endlessly discussed and treated to a variety of interpretations. It was also agreed that Mr Alexander was soon to acquire both a wife and a fortune.

And Annie hazarded a guess that there would be a Dovewood wedding before the year was out.

"It's no secret that Mr Alexander's scarce ever at home these days," said Annie. "He's not even at the Readings and that speaks for itself. And the Mistress has told me—"

"The Missus has no liking for being put right," said Clara. "And I dare say is glad enough as he stays away. I dare say she tell the Master she were affronted."

"You may dare say anything you choose, Clara," said Annie. "But I know what I know. It's certain that Mr Alexander's young lady has at least twenty thousand pounds of her own, and she the only child of a rich papa. Now there's the clock striking and another hower gone.

Death is nearer
Heaven is dearer,
Let me see my duty clearer!"

"One of these days, Annie," said Clara, "you'll see your duty so clear your eyes'll pop out of your head. And then where'll you be? You'll not be able to peek and peer no more."

At night Betony tucked her red cloak over the thin blankets and slept until Annie woke her at five minutes to six. Betony dreaded the moment of waking. Annie would knock softly and then fling open the door. Standing behind her flickering candle she was like some staring, malignant spectre. Once she said, "You know I'm watching you, Betsy, don't you? You know I'm watching you? You gave me the creeps when I first saw you – and you still do. I think you're a child of the devil, Betsy. What are you doing here?"

"Earning a few honest shillings," said Betony.

On some mornings the water was frozen hard in Betony's jug and she dressed, shivering, under her cloak while the candlelight twinkled on the dark frosted window. Then she put on the old black petticoat and was thankful for the extra warmth.

Katharine did not come.

Mrs Rock continued calmly to direct the housework, to give orders to the tradesmen, to check the linen and issue the tea, sugar and candles. She continued to sit at the head of the table during the first part of the servants' dinner with the cook on her right hand and Annie on her left. But she ate her other meals in her parlour. There was little conversation when Mrs Rock was in the kitchen but as soon as the door had closed behind her, Clara came into her own.

For Clara every day held the possibility of delight. A pedlar or fortune-teller might knock on the area door, an organ-grinder might visit the street and grind out a tinkling tune while his polite monkey doffed his hat and collected the pennies. Or, best of all, her soldier might appear and pause to admire the Dovewood cakes while she chanced to be cleaning the Dovewood windows.

The Dovewood windows were kept in a state of permanent brilliance.

Herb Gerard

20

Alexander

Betony woke unwillingly. Down in the alley the old Charley was calling the time. "Half-past two o'clock and a clear and frosty morning!"

Betony heard him every night and usually fell asleep again at once. His thin, quavering voice had become as familiar to her as the desolate sighing of the night wind over the London chimneys. Through frost, rain and fog he limped on his beat, small, decrepit and indomitable. Once Betony had slipped out of bed and had caught a glimpse of him as he came down the alley with the light of his lantern wavering along the wall beside him. He must have sensed that she was at the garret window because he had looked up and raised his staff in greeting. Then he had limped on.

"Half past two o'clock and a clear and frosty morning!"

Betony was wide awake now, awake and resentful. The old Charley had dragged her out of a dream of Number 26, and of Linny. Linny had been watching for her at the shop door and had cried, "Why doesn't Betony come home?" And Jacob from the shadows of the shop, had answered, "B-but B-Betony's not at home yet anywhere. Not at home – not at home."

Half past two o'clock—

The old Charley's voice was dwindling away.

I must go to sleep again, thought Betony.

There was a sudden crash below, followed by a brief silence. Then Betony heard the creak of Alexander's door. She stiffened and forgot her dream. Alexander must have been in his bed on the other side, for hours. But there was somebody in his study.

Betony listened, holding her breath, and finally sat up.

I must tell Mrs Rock, she thought, and she'll fetch Mr Dovewood.

The floor boards were like ice under her feet as she fumbled for her shoes. She pulled her cloak off the bed and wrapped herself in it. Then, trembling, she felt her way down the garret stairs.

Alexander's lamp was alight and his door was ajar. Betony hesitated. She wondered wildly if she should, herself, creep through the arch and wake the Master or Mr Alexander. But as she stood irresolute the door was flung open and Alexander himself appeared.

"Oh!" said Betony. "Oh! I thought—" she stopped.

Alexander was staring at her with an expression of incredulity.

"You?" he said. "You? But you did not tell me that you would come."

And to Betony's astonishment, he caught her hand and kissed it.

Then Betony saw his face change.

"But you are not Miss Fernley," he said.

"I know I'm not," said Betony.

"I beg your pardon," said Alexander. "I trust that you will believe – will believe—"

"It's all right," said Betony. "I know the kiss wasn't meant for me."

"Your resemblance to the young lady that – that I spoke of is quite extraordinary," said Alexander. "And the red cloak—"

"It's all right," said Betony again.

"Miss Fernley is a very dear friend," said Alexander. "I have known her since she was a little schoolgirl. She is, indeed, the dearest friend that I have."

"I'm supposed to be like another girl," said Betony. "My face seems to be in pretty general use. I'll go back to bed now. I'm glad you aren't a burglar."

She was still trembling. "I'm Betsy," she said. "One of Mrs Dovewood's housemaids. Good night – Sir."

"Wait," said Alexander. "Your garret must be like an ice-house on a night like this. And you sound half perished with cold. You had best warm yourself by my fire while I make some tea. I was working late and kicked over a bucket when I crossed the room to put the kettle on the fire. Since you failed to catch a thief, you must not be permitted to catch a cold. One sneeze, in the presence of Mrs Dovewood, and you would find yourself out in the street. I should not wish to be the cause of such a disaster. Our last Betsy was dismissed for daring to cough on a foggy morning."

"What about all this water on the floor?" said Betony.

"I was going down to the basement to look for a cloth," said Alexander, "but I changed my mind because I feared to alarm the footman who sleeps in the pantry. The water can be left to dry."

He moved the only chair from the table to the fire.

"Sit down and warm yourself," he said. "The kettle is near boiling. This is, of course, highly irregular, and would be compromising in the eyes of the world. But I assure you that you have nothing to fear. I want only to preserve you from dismissal."

"Thank you," said Betony, and added, "Sir."

There was a glowing fire and the room was warm. The table had been dragged away from the window and nearer to the hearth, and a sketchbook lay open on it, together with paints and brushes, a magnifying glass and a jar of water. Under the lamp there was a single head of groundsel in a small bottle.

Betony glanced down at the sketchbook. Alexander had been making a detailed study of the groundsel, and there were notes down both sides of the page.

"*Senecio vulgaris*," said Alexander. "It obligingly blooms at all times of the year. And there are a great number of species."

"Are you a botanist?" asked Betony.

"I cannot yet aspire to that noble title," said Alexander and smiled.

And Betony was aware of his happiness. It seemed to brighten the air about him as he stooped to lift the kettle.

She sat down.

"Most of what I know of plants I have learned from one old parson," said Alexander. "I ride out to his country parsonage as often as I can and bring back my trophies to record in my book or press for my albums. Although," he added, "a pressed specimen is but a poor substitute for a living plant. Now where is my teapot?"

"Behind the lamp," said Betony.

She had stopped trembling.

"Clara can't imagine what you do with all your 'weeds'," she said.

"I keep my book and albums locked in that chest," said Alexander. "I have no wish for my botanical studies to cause any sort of trouble for my father. He knows what I am about and is willing enough for me to continue. But Mrs Dovewood has made her own plans, without reference to me, and—"

"Yes," said Betony. "I quite understand."

"I cannot think why I am speaking to you so openly," said Alexander. "I must beg you not to divulge—"

"Of course I won't," said Betony.

Alexander poured a little water into the teapot and set the kettle back on the trivet. Then he stood looking down at her.

"There is something strange about you, Betsy," he said, "I knew it when I touched your hand. It is not only that your manner of speech is curious and that there is a certain pleasant simplicity in your deportment. Where are you come from?"

"If I told you, you wouldn't believe me," said Betony.

"Now *there* you are mistaken," said Alexander. "I can believe anything at a quarter to three in the morning. I should not even be greatly astonished if, at this moment, you were to vanish from my chair."

"I could," said Betony. "But I won't."

"At least tell me your name," said Alexander. "You may do that with the most perfect assurance that I shall believe you. I have always disliked the labelling of our maids with an A, B or C."

"The teapot must be quite warm enough by now," said Betony. "And the kettle's boiling."

"I recollect your voice," said Alexander. "And yet I would swear that I have never conversed with you before."

"An old Charley pinned your coat to my cloak on Twelfth Night," said Betony. "And I said 'Thank you'."

"Ah," said Alexander. "So you were the modest young lady from the country whose face I never saw."

"Yes," said Betony. "Only I wasn't from the country."

Alexander was still gazing down at her. "You are, perhaps, come from a greater distance?" he said.

"Yes," said Betony. "Shall I make the tea?"

"No," said Alexander. "But when you have drunk my tea you will, perhaps, permit me to conjecture—"

"I can't prevent you from conjecturing," said Betony.

Alexander laughed. "Then I shall make the tea immediately," he said.

21

The Wind Against the Wind

"Here is the sugar," said Alexander. "I regret that I have no cream to offer you."

"And your cup?" said Betony.

"The painting jar will serve," said Alexander. "Now, as to my conjecture—"

"I came to oblige Mrs Rock," said Betony.

"As to my conjecture," said Alexander, "you are sheathed, as it were, in an air that is different from ours. I suspect that you are come from a distance that cannot be measured in miles."

"Am I?" said Betony.

Alexander emptied his painting water into the nearest bucket and filled the jar with tea. Then he sat down on the chest, which stood against the wall on the far side of the hearth.

"I think, Betsy, that you belong neither to this place nor this time," he said.

"Don't I?" said Betony. She sipped her tea and Alexander sipped his.

"You're happy, aren't you?" said Betony. "I've a little cousin who has the same capacity for joy. She's nine years old and she's called Linny – Linaria."

"And you?" said Alexander.

"I work and sleep," said Betony. "And dream of another Dovewood shop."

"Your little cousin has a pretty name," said Alexander. "I have sometimes thought that if I were ever blessed with a son and daughter I should name them after plants

— always, of course, with their mamma's approval. I myself was named after an emperor. Ridiculous! Now where is this other shop that you dream about?"

"It's some distance from here," said Betony. "At least — it will be."

"Hah!" said Alexander. "So my conjecture—"

Betony laughed. She was warm now, and at ease. The long-legged Alexander inspired perfect trust.

"I should have guessed that you were the 'mad horti-culturist'," she said. "But the word 'mad' doesn't apply any longer."

"You speak in riddles," said Alexander. "And no man can be expected to guess a riddle at this time in the morning. But between midnight and dawn a man can believe in any marvel. So tell me, where is this other shop?"

Betony put her tea cup down in the hearth. Then she felt in the pocket of her cloak and handed Alexander the little calendar that Aunt Maple had sent her.

"That's my proper time," said Betony.

She was conscious of overwhelming relief. For a few short, blessed moments she could be herself, Betony Dovewood. She was sharply aware of her own identity, for perhaps the first time in her life. And she was aware too of the time to which she belonged. For a moment the lamplit room wavered like a reflection in water.

Alexander had got up and was examining the calendar under the lamp. She heard him give a sharp exclamation, and then he was silent as he turned the tiny pages. Betony's vision steadied. Alexander glanced at her and then returned to the calendar.

"I have known all kinds of miracles," he said at last. "Indeed, the world of nature is a world of miracles. But this, even at three o'clock in the morning, is the strangest miracle that I ever met with. So many years between us! And such perfect proof! And here you sit. And here am I."

"Yes," said Betony.

"But there is a second, even greater miracle," said Alexander. "The name that is written in this little almanac – the name of Betony Dovewood."

"I'd forgotten that Aunt Maple had written my name in it," said Betony. "She's so proud of being a Dovewood she writes the word whenever she can."

"Betony!" said Alexander. "*Stachy betonica*. It has purple flowers."

"Yes," said Betony.

"I believe, Cousin, that I should pour us each a second cup of tea," said Alexander.

"Cousin?" said Betony.

"Cousin, is a comfortable word," said Alexander. "It covers a multiplicity of relationships. Now hand me your cup and tell me your story."

So Betony told him.

Alexander put more coal on the fire.

"I have a thousand questions to ask," he said. "But let us consider Time. You do not belong to this time. And yet here you are. So we will consider what Time is."

"It's too complicated," said Betony. "Much too complicated."

"We will simplify it," said Alexander. "We will consider Time as a wind. And sometimes it is a great gale and sometimes a slow-moving current of air. But it blows us all away – in time."

"Time is usually thought of as water," said Betony. "*Time like an ever-rolling stream—*"

"But since Time is neither wind nor water we can make it whichever we choose," said Alexander. "Can I persuade you, Cousin, to regard Time as a wind?"

"All right," said Betony. "It's a wind. I'm too sleepy to argue."

Alexander stood up.

"I am forgetful," he said. "You must finish your night's sleep."

"But I'm glad to be myself for a little," said Betony. "Let me stay a few more minutes. Tell me about Time."

"I have stood under a tree in autumn," said Alexander, "and watched the leaves blowing all one way. But sometimes I have seen how a single leaf will fly back against the wind as though some truant gust had caught it, and that single leaf will turn and twist until it is snatched back into the main current of air."

"Spurrey spoke of the wind against the wind," said Betony.

"Perhaps you are that solitary leaf, Cousin?"

"Perhaps," said Betony. "But that doesn't take the china cottage into acount."

"A harmless agent," said Alexander. "The cottage set the truant gust blowing. There, I have offered you a perfect explanation of your presence, by my fire, on this February morning! My new theory of Time has never been made public *only* because I have but just devised it. Now since there is still some water in the kettle, I will make some fresh tea."

"Your tea is better than your reasoning," said Betony.

But she was asleep when Alexander brought her the tea.

22

Annie

She dreamed of Jacob. He came into the shop and the bell clanged and, as usual, went on clanging. But she was the bell. And she was being shaken. She put out a protesting hand and Alexander's voice said, "You must wake, Cousin. It is near six o'clock and the virtuous Annie will be knocking on your door in a few minutes."

"Yes," said Betony. "Yes. I was dreaming of the other shop."

She had reached the top of the attic stairs when she heard Annie's voice below.

"Good morning, Sir. I didn't expect, Sir, that you'd be up so early. I have to wake that Betsy, Sir, if you'll be so good as to let me pass."

"You may save yourself the trouble," said Alexander briskly. "Betsy is already up. I kicked over a bucket and she feared that some thief was broken in, and came down to see. You will be good enough to fetch a cloth and mop the floor."

"Yes, Sir," said Annie. "It was that Clara who cleaned your study, Sir, the last time. I tell her all her duty belongs to the Mistress but she pays no more heed to me than to a soapbubble floating in the air. I'm mostly occupied with needlework for the Mistress these days, Sir, but I'll fetch a cloth since you give the order. Will Betsy be up in her garret, Sir, or gone down?"

"I believe that she is still upstairs," said Alexander.

"She's a quiet one, that Betsy," said Annie. "I've watched her, Sir, and in a manner of speaking there's something underhand about her. I'd hazard a guess, Sir, she's not what she seems. The first time that ever I saw her my heart seemed to stop, Sir, and my feet and hands went icy cold. But I keep my eye on her, Sir, against my will, as it were."

"It's not your duty to judge your fellow servants," said Alexander sharply. "Or to keep an eye on them."

"No, Sir," said Annie. "But there's times, Sir, when a word of warning—"

The clock on Mrs Rock's landing struck six.

"Now there's another hower gone," said Annie.

"Death is nearer
Heaven is dearer—"

Betony slipped into her garret and softly closed the door.

23

The Rural Young Lady

"Pray be seated, Cousin," said Alexander.

"If I sit down I shan't have time to do the room properly," said Betony. "And there's something that I must ask you."

"You shall ask nothing until you are seated," said Alexander. "You are somewhat pale, Cousin."

"For these last few nights I've not slept well," said Betony.

"Then you shall rest now, and later I will sweep and dust," said Alexander. "I must tell you that I requested Mrs Rock to send only you to my study because only you had a proper respect for my buckets."

"Annie is still talking about that bucket you kicked over," said Betony.

She sat down and Alexander closed the door.

"During the past week," he said, "the industrious Annie has discovered that it is her duty not only to bring up my coals (which the footman should carry) but also to deliver innumerable jugs of water and innumerable short sermons. I am being warned against you, Cousin. Annie appears to be in constant consultation with her conscience, and I am uneasy for you. I cannot understand why Mrs Rock permits that young woman—"

"Annie is very useful to Mrs Dovewood," said Betony.

"Then Annie is safe enough," said Alexander. "And we had best change the subject. You spoke of something you wished to ask me, but I have so many questions to put to you that I scarce know where to begin."

"May I ask my question first," said Betony.

"You may ask anything, Cousin," said Alexander.

"My question is about Miss Fernley," said Betony. "I've been thinking and thinking and—"

"If I answer your question," said Alexander, "it is only because I trust you. In the present circumstances caution is necessary. Miss Fernley's future – and, I believe, her happiness, together with mine – depends on secrecy. Will you give me your word, Cousin, not to speak of Miss Fernley to anyone."

"Yes," said Betony.

"Then ask your question, Cousin," said Alexander.

"What is Miss Fernley's Christian name?" said Betony.

Alexander began to laugh.

"Now that is a short, simple question," he said. "And the most easy to answer. Miss Fernley's Christian name is Katharine."

"Oh dear!" said Betony. "Oh, dear!"

"What have I said, Cousin, that could possibly disturb you?" cried Alexander. "I have always considered Katharine one of the most agreeable names in the world."

"I should have guessed," said Betony. "I *should* have guessed. Please tell me about Katharine."

"She is like you, and yet not like you," said Alexander. "Indeed I marvel that I ever mistook you for Katharine. There is a sort of directness in your manner whereas Katharine is timid and shy. She appears to me as beautiful as an angel and yet is all innocence. Her life has not been over-happy and she is for ever fearful, and apprehensive of the future. If you bid me speak of Katharine, Cousin, I shall never be done."

"Then please go on," said Betony.

Alexander began to pace about the room. "The first time that ever I saw Katharine was in the spring, when I

99

was a boy of seventeen," he said. "Mrs Rock had noted my interest in the weeds that grew in our untended garden, and spoke of a certain village where the parson was so ardent a botanist that he had made a garden of common country plants, which he tended with all the devotion that other men give to their rich, hot-house blooms. And the tale delighted me, especially when Mrs Rock added, in her grim way, that the parson was reported to love his simple plants rather more than he loved his simple parishioners."

"Go on," said Betony.

"The village was not too far distant from London," said Alexander, "so what must I do but ride out to see the parson's garden for myself. I had no hesitation in introducing myself to the parson, and if he felt any surprise at the sudden arrival of an unknown youth, he did not show it. He merely set aside the sermon he was writing and ushered me out into his garden. And there we stayed until his sister fetched us in to dinner. There is a certain freemasonry among botanists, Cousin, that is as rare as it is delightful."

"But Katharine?" said Betony.

"Now the parson's sister," said Alexander, "seemed to me the most sensible and learned woman I had ever met. And, indeed, I still hold to that opinion. She had received some legacy from her godfather and, having no wish to change her habits or remove from the parsonage, where she kept house for her brother, she had endowed a school with the money. And as I rode away from the parsonage I saw the thirteen little schoolgirls running out of school, all in their red cloaks like bright field poppies."

"Go on," said Betony.

"I reined in my horse to let the children cross the road," said Alexander, "and twelve of them curtsied and hurried away across the fields. But Katharine was the last of them and she hesitated behind the school gate. She was but ten years old at that time, and painfully timid. To put her at her ease I told her that I had ridden from London. And I said that I had never seen so many primroses. In truth they were everywhere, under the hedges and in the woods. Then Katharine came out from behind the gate and picked me a single primrose and handed it up to me without a word. And I still have it."

"Did you tell Mrs Rock that you'd seen the little school-girls?" asked Betony.

"I gave Mrs Rock an account of all that had occurred," said Alexander, "and received, to my amazement, a fierce rebuke. I was at fault, she said to single out the girl, because a poor village child should not be given cause to think more highly of herself than her situation warranted. Up till that moment, Cousin, Mrs Rock and I had been friends. Indeed, I had come to regard her as an ally. But from then on she treated me with the cold unbending formality that exists between servant and master. And I could at no time find my way back into her good graces. So I never spoke to her of all my other visits to the parson and his sister. Nor of our botanical excursions through the woods and meadows. And I never spoke to her of Katharine although I soon discovered, from the child's talk, that Mrs Rock had been a friend of her mother's and a benefactor to her."

"But listen!" said Betony. "Listen! Don't you think that now Mrs Rock should be told how – how things are?"

"No, Cousin, I do not," said Alexander. "Mrs Rock has been generous, and always concerned for Katharine's health, but there has been a strictness, a sort of cold constraint about her behaviour which has intimidated Katharine. When Katharine first understood that Mrs Rock was housekeeper here, the poor child was greatly distressed because she feared that Mrs Rock might put an end to that confidence and friendship that had grown up between us. Katharine reveres Mrs Rock and is grateful for her continuing benevolence, but yet cannot love her."

"But hasn't Katharine *ever* spoken of you to Mrs Rock?" asked Betony.

"I believe that lately Katharine has written of me in vague terms to Mrs Rock," said Alexander. "But my poor Kate has always been tongue-tied in Mrs Rock's presence and has never been able to confide in her as she might have done in her own mother. Now Katharine and I have come to a perfect understanding and—"

"And you must tell Mrs Rock," said Betony. "You *must*, Alexander."

Alexander stopped pacing. "No, Cousin," he said. "Oh no! Katharine is an orphan and has no relative or guardian to whom she owes her duty. But she is assured that Mrs Rock would prevent our plans if she knew of them. Indeed, during these recent weeks Katharine has been in a state of strange disquiet but refuses to tell me the cause."

"But listen—" said Betony.

"It is you who must listen, Cousin," said Alexander. "It is not only Mrs Rock that we have to fear. My step-mamma is determined that I shall marry some genteel heiress. My father, you see – it is all planned – is to purchase an estate for me so the name of Dovewood will be numbered among the country families. My step-mamma's ambition, Cousin, goes hand in hand with her romantic imagination. But she has, besides a most violent and tyrannical will."

"I know," said Betony. "But—"

"Consider, Cousin," said Alexander. "If my step-mamma were to discover, through Mrs Rock, that the rural young lady, to whom I have given my heart, possesses nothing in all the world but that same heart, together with her own beauty, delicacy and tenderness, why then there would be such a prolonged and dreadful convulsion in the household that my father's life would be made intolerable. Because I am his son, he would be subjected to endless dramatic performances, to torrents of reproaches and avalanches of resentment. And I should have no alternative but openly to defy Mrs Dovewood and, possibly, my father, as well."

"I see that," said Betony. "But—"

"There would also be a danger to Mrs Rock herself," said Alexander. "If my step-mamma, discovered that Mrs Rock had been Katharine's friend then Mrs Rock would instantly be thrust out into the street, her living gone and her character blackened. No, no, Cousin. My affairs must remain secret until they are concluded."

Betony remembered Mrs Rock's quiet, desperate weeping.

"But," she said, "surely, it would be possible—"

There was a knock on the door and Betony stood up quickly. Alexander handed her the broom. Then he opened the door.

Annie was outside. She curtsied hurriedly. "I supposed that you'd be gone out, Sir," she said.

"As you see – I am still here," said Alexander.

"Yes, Sir," said Annie. "And Betsy has to help that Clara sweep the carpets with tea-leaves. The carpets are always done with tea-leaves once a fortnight, Sir. Will Betsy be long?"

"No," said Alexander.

"I've still the dusting to do," said Betony.

24

Warning on the Stairs

It was growing late. Betony sat on her bed with her cloak clutched tightly round her. She had not undressed. Her candle was still burning and she had forgotten to shut her door.

Below, on Mrs Rock's landing, the clock struck eleven. If I knew what to do, I'd do it, thought Betony, but I don't know.

She shivered.

I could still go home, she thought. I could think of the crack and vanish. I could have breakfast tomorrow morning with Linny and Spurrey and Gerard. And Jacob might come into the shop. But I can't go home, yet. One has to finish – to finish – the things one has begun. One can't shelve responsibilities.

She remembered Alexander's face as he strode about his bare study. He had warmed her with his own happiness, and trusted her. He had called her "Cousin" and given her a sense of her own identity."

If only I knew what to do, thought Betony.

There were quick steps on the stairs and Mrs Rock slipped into the garret.

"I saw your light," she said. "You should be in your bed."

She hesitated, and Betony saw that she was struggling to control her agitation.

"Katharine is come at last," she said. "She is come!" She closed the garret door and leaned against it. "I can still scarce believe it," said Mrs Rock. "I looked out of

my parlour window and she was standing in the street –
even as you stood on Twelfth Night. I ran down, and
brought her in, and shall keep her close until she is fully
recovered. She is in a highly nervous state and greatly
fatigued."

"But how—?" began Betony.

"She will sleep on my sofa tonight and remain in my
bedchamber during the day," said Mrs Rock.

"Fortunately no one saw her arrive. I would not, for
the world, have Annie suspect—"

"But you may safely tell Alexander," said Betony.

"Are you mad?" said Mrs Rock. "Why should the
young Master be told of Katharine's arrival? It is no
concern of his. I thought it right to inform you. You will
soon be free, but until then you will remain silent. I trust
you recollect your promise that you will never speak of
what you know."

"Yes," said Betony, "but—"

"You are wasting the candle. And will be unfit for
work tomorrow," said Mrs Rock harshly. "I cannot have
you yawning at the Reading. Now get to bed."

"Listen!" said Betony. "Please, listen!"

But Mrs Rock had closed the door and was gone.

The next morning Annie did not climb the garret
stairs or knock on the garret door. And her forgetfulness
caused Betony a strange uneasiness. She had scarcely slept
all night and had got up early. The thought of Katharine
hidden below in Mrs Rock's parlour, haunted Betony.

The Reading was prolonged. Mrs Dovewood's heroine
was nearing the end of her search and there seemed some
prospect that the poem, too, would come to an end.
Betony, watching the Mistress declaiming behind her
pens, inks and papers, was aware that she herself was
being watched. Annie had turned a little and was

regarding her with smiling malice. It was the first time that Betony had seen the woman smile. Afterwards, in the hall, Annie brushed against her as the other servants were dispersing. Mrs Rock had already disappeared.

"I've a few words to say to you, Betsy," said Annie.

"Be quick then," said Betony. "I have to help Clara with the beds."

Annie followed her up the stairs.

"You won't be assisting that Clara much longer," she said. "I heard you this morning, Betsy. I heard you."

"What did you hear?" asked Betony.

"I heard you conversing in Mr Alexander's study before the clock struck six," said Annie.

"But I wasn't—" began Betony, and left the sentence unfinished.

Katharine! she thought. It must surely have been Katharine.

"You needn't say that you wasn't in the study," said Annie, "because the lie won't do you no good. There are those that fall down dead if they utter a lie and there are those that are let to lie and lie, so the devil's fires are kept blazing with wicked words like flaming oil. And so it is with you."

"I didn't know," said Betony. "Is that all you want to say?"

"It's not all," said Annie. "And it's my duty that holds me here and not any wish of mine. From the first, Betsy, you made my blood run cold, like, in a manner of speaking, as I'd seen a ghost. But I kept my eyes on you. You never let out no information as to where you came from and, to this day, there's not a soul that knows your true name. Oh no, Betsy! You'll not push past me. You'll stay until I've spoke the warning my conscience bids me speak."

"Well, hurry up your conscience then," said Betony.

"I'll take all the time I need," said Annie. "And you'd better pay attention. I heard you, Betsy, talking with Mr Alexander, like you talked before. And as to that water that the young Master ordered me to mop up – it was half dry, Betsy, before I came to it with my cloth. So the bucket must have been tipped over in the early howers. And there was that tea cup and the jar as well, Betsy, with tea leaves in them both. And all that I noted, Betsy, but I held my tongue."

"I wonder why," said Betony.

"Then," said Annie, "when you should have been cleaning Mr Alexander's study, there was more conversing. But I kept a still tongue in my head."

"Why?" said Betony.

"I'll tell you for why," said Annie. "I'll tell you for why. The Mistress was so took up with her writings she weren't ready to listen. And I know the Mistress, Betsy. I have to choose my time, Betsy, like I was attending on some heartless great crocodile as would snap me up, in an instant, and never heed my groans."

She spoke with extraordinary violence.

"I have to keep my place, Betsy, because there's none as'll care for me when I'm old. I have to save every penny I can get. And I only speak freely to you now, Betsy, because you'll be out of a place tomorrow, and gone from here."

"Your life must be pretty miserable," said Betony. "I'm sorry."

"You may save your dolorations," said Annie fiercely. "The Mistress has told me that her poem will be finished today. And tomorrow, Betsy, after the Reading, I'll tell her all I've seen and heard. And the words spoke this morning, Betsy, before six o'clock, will mean as you're sent off. And Mrs Rock won't save you. And you'll get no character. And you'll get no wages."

Her voice rose. "And you'll be tramping the London streets tomorrow, Betsy, with no place nor any hopes of one. So you'd best pack your box."

"I hadn't realised you hated me so much," said Betony.

"I've hated you from the first moment I set eyes on you," said Annie. "And when I heard you say this morning, 'I had to come, Alex,' then I knew that my conscience hadn't been mistook in warning me you were a child of the Devil. But tomorrow this house'll be free of you. Oh, yes! And you won't never come back. Never! Never! Never!"

Her voice had risen to a screech but suddenly she turned and scurried away down the stairs.

Great Maple or Sycamore

25

The Plan

Betony stood still.

I must talk to Alexander, she thought, I must tell him—

Then Mrs Rock came quickly through the arch on the landing.

"The young Master has been down to me," she said. "He is rearranging his books and wishes you to dust them before he puts them back on the shelves. You *should* be making the beds."

"Yes, Ma'am," said Betony.

"Did I hear Annie's voice?"

"Yes, Ma'am," said Betony. "Annie's conscience—"

"She was right to reprove you for wasting time," said

Mrs Rock. "I will tell Clara that you will be occupied for the next hour."

She caught Betony's arm. "You recollect your promise."

"Yes," said Betony.

Alexander's table was piled with books, but Alexander himself was staring up at the wind-blown London smoke.

He turned quickly as Betony slipped into the study. "Katharine is come, Cousin," he said.

"I know," said Betony.

"How can you know?" said Alexander, "Katharine is being kept hidden."

"Annie heard Katharine talking to you this morning and thought I was with you," said Betony.

Alexander began to pace about the room. "My poor Kate is in great distress," he said. "And as for me – I am in need of advice, Cousin. It is a question now – or later – of persuading Katharine, of making plans."

"Things seem to have got rather complicated," said Betony. "D'you want me to dust the books?"

"No," said Alexander. "The books – I had to do something – so much is at stake. You are kind and have great good sense, Cousin, so I thought—"

"Couldn't you stop tramping about," said Betony.

Alexander placed the chair near the fire for her and sat down on the chest.

"I only learned this morning that Mrs Rock had decided that Katharine was to come here as a housemaid," he said. "My poor Kate was allowed *no* say in the matter and has made herself sick with anxiety. She says she cannot play a part in my presence. She says she dreads Mrs Rock's authority and constant watchfulness."

"Why didn't she tell you before?" asked Betony.

"That is what I asked," said Alexander. "It seems that my dear Kate remained silent because she could not endure the thought of forcing me into any premature action. She has a mind of great delicacy and sensibility. She hoped, too, that Mrs Rock would change her mind or find some other housemaid."

"I see," said Betony.

"Mrs Rock, however, did not change her mind," said Alexander. "She wrote a final, peremptory letter and threatened to take the coach and fetch Katharine to London herself. So then my poor Kate came to me."

"I see," said Betony.

"While Kate lived quietly in the village I hesitated to – to take the final step because of my father, and because of all the trouble such a step would cause him," said Alexander. "But now Katharine finds herself in an intolerable situation. And yet she begs me to wait. You must understand, Cousin, that I would not, for all the world, press her too far. She fears Mrs Rock and yet would not alienate me from my father. And, as for me, my thoughts veer like the wind. In short, Cousin—"

And Alexander got up and began to pace about the room again.

"I came here to take Katharine's place for a short time," said Betony, "but tomorrow morning, after the Reading, Annie will see to it that I'm dismissed. So, whatever Mrs Rock wishes, Katharine will not be able to stay here because we're supposed to be the same person."

Alexander had stopped dead.

"So the matter is already settled," he said.

"Yes," said Betony.

"Cousin," said Alexander, "my very dear Cousin, you have lifted such a weight from my mind that I know not how to thank you. Now I know what I must do. Now Katharine herself will be convinced. Now the pious Annie has performed an act of real charity – which would doubtless horrify her were she to comprehend it. Will you assist me, Cousin?"

"Assist?" said Betony.

"Katharine is to spend today in Mrs Rock's bed-chamber, and will sleep tonight on the sofa in Mrs Rock's parlour. She is always instructed to lock herself in," said Alexander. "But tonight we will slip away. I have a married friend whose wife will care for Katharine. And after we are married we will return to the village."

"And Mrs Rock?" said Betony.

"Katharine shall write her a note," said Alexander. "And I will write to my father. And when my step-mamma understands that neither of them is guilty of any complicity in the business she will have no cause to blame either."

He smiled. "Doubtless Mrs Dovewood will express her disapprobation," he said. "But there will be no scapegoats. And you, Cousin, will be free to return to the other shop and your own time."

"Yes," said Betony. "What do you want me to do?"

"See us on our way tonight – or rather, at two o'clock tomorrow morning," said Alexander. "We shall go out through the shop and you will bolt the alley door when we are gone. The Bucks are often about at night and would wreck the shop if they got in."

"I see," said Betony. "You will need to talk to Katharine. The best time will be when we are all at dinner. Mrs Rock eats the first course with us."

"You are my most kind and careful Cousin," said Alexander. "And I cannot conceive what I should have done without you."

"Thank you," said Betony.

She was close to tears.

26

Escape down the Alley

It was a wild night. Towering, smoky clouds drove across the moon, sometimes hiding it altogether and sometimes drawing apart so that it shone down on the London streets in white splendour. At ten minutes to two Betony was wrapped in her cloak and ready with her candle alight; at one minute to two she picked up the candle and crept down the garret stairs.

Alexander came out of his study leaving the door ajar. He carried a lighted lantern and wore his great coat. His tall hat was tucked under his arm. He smiled at Betony and they went on down the stairs. Katharine was waiting outside Mrs Rock's parlour.

The hood of her red cloak was pulled over her head so Betony caught only a glimpse of her face. One after another they stole on.

If a stair creaked they stood still to listen but heard only the wind and the sound of their own quick breathing.

The door into the shop was locked but the key was in the lock. Alexander turned the key softly and opened the door.

They crept into the shop, behind the long counters. Betony was aware that Katharine was trembling. The great mirrors on the walls flung back the lantern light and endlessly reflected the small flame of Betony's candle. But the shop was a cave of shadows, peopled on all sides by their own tiptoeing shades who moved with them and the moving lights. Betony put out her hand and touched Katharine's arm.

"I sold buns here on Twelfth Night," she whispered.

And Katharine murmured, "Thank you," as though the commonplace word "buns" had reassured her, and she were grateful.

Alexander was already unbolting the side door. He swung it open and Betony put down her candle on the bun table.

Then Katharine pushed back her hood and Betony saw a pallid, dark-eyed girl who smiled uncertainly as she held out her hand.

"The other face," said Betony. "But we're not really alike because you're so pretty."

She took Katharine's hand in both of hers. It was small and very cold. "Everything will be all right," said Betony. "You've no need to be afraid. Everything will be all right."

"We must go," said Alexander. "The two letters, Cousin, are on my table. Will you make sure that my father and Mrs Rock receive them?"

"Yes," said Betony.

Alexander looked down at her. "Somewhere, Cousin," he said, "I believe that we shall meet again – in some sweet grove, perhaps, where the wind of Time no longer blows."

He stooped and kissed her hand. "That," he said, "is for no one but you, Cousin."

Betony watched them as they walked away down the alley. Alexander regulating his long stride to Katharine's shorter steps. The moon had emerged from a black cloud and Betony saw that Alexander had given Katharine his arm. They moved as one, Katharine's cloak lifting a little in the wind and the lantern swinging from Alexander's hand.

Betony watched them until they were out of sight.

27

The Bucks

There seemed to Betony no reason why she should move, why she should tiptoe through the empty shop and up the stairs, why she should creep into her cold bed.

She thought suddenly: Nothing I have done here will make the smallest difference to the future. Nothing I may still do is of the least importance. This is not my time. But I'm still Betony Dovewood.

The dark, tumbled clouds were still driving up the sky. One cloud, fringed with silver, had thrust across the moon's face. A few drops of rain pattered on the cobbles.

But Betony still stood outside the shop. I shall deliver the letters and then go home, she thought. Linny will be pleased. Dear Linny! And so will Spurrey. And Jacob will be glad to see me.

A spark of light showed far down the alley and she heard the old Charley's voice, carried faintly on the wind.

"Half past two o'clock and a cloudy, moonlight morning!"

She waited, watching the light as it flickered nearer. She had no idea that she had been standing so long. The old Charley was visible now, a humble, plodding figure in his long coat and battered hat. He came on steadily, the light from his lantern jerking along the alley wall and glinting on the wet cobbles.

I'll wait and say goodbye to him, thought Betony. It'll be strange not to hear him calling in the night.

The sound of distant shouting startled her. As the gusts of wind drove towards her she heard a babel of voices and laughter. Betony saw the old Charley pause and glance over his shoulder. Then he hobbled on.

Far down the alley lights appeared and fresh shouting broke out. "The fox! The old fox! View halloa!" A crowd of Bucks were straggling down the alley waving their hats and baying like hounds. It was clear that they had been drinking and were eager for any sport.

"The fox! The old fox!"

Betony stood trembling on the wet cobbles. She was horrified but unable to move.

"View halloa! The fox! The fox!"

The old Charley was making desperate efforts to hurry.

To Betony the windy night had become a nightmare. She could see the leader of the Bucks now, a stout florid young man whose lantern swung wildly as he charged forward.

The old Charley still came on. But he seemed exhausted.

"View halloa! The fox is ours, boys! We have him – the old fox!"

The Charley had put his lantern down and backed against the wall. Perhaps he still hoped that the Bucks would pass him by. Pity for the old man and fierce anger took hold of Betony.

She began to run,

After that all was confusion.

She tried to seize the old Charley's staff to defend him, but he held on to it. And the Bucks were only a few yards away. She saw their faces, grinning and dissolute, in the wavering lantern light as the old man fended her off. Then suddenly he let the staff go and she lurched backwards. The staff flew out of her hands and under the feet of the leading Buck. He stumbled and his lantern whirled away and splintered against the wall. He tried to regain his balance, stumbled a second time and crashed full length on the cobbles.

And his friends fell over him. One after another, unable to halt their lumbering charge, they went down like dominoes between the alley walls, roaring and cursing as they fell.

Betony picked up the old Charley's lantern and caught his arm.

"Come on," she said.

The Bucks were still struggling on the cobbles. They appeared to be too drunk to get to their feet and had begun to fight each other. It was now raining heavily.

"Wild and wicked, them Bucks," said the old Charley. "You should ha' gone inside, Miss Bet."

"I couldn't," said Betony.

"I didn't understand as you was atrying to help," said the old man. "Now where's me staff?"

The staff had been kicked several yards and Betony retrieved it. One of the Bucks had lurched to his feet but was promptly pulled down by his fellows.

"Come on!" cried Betony.

"This rain'll cool 'em," said the old Charley. "Maybe I could get me breath back in the shop?"

"Yes," said Betony. Her candle was still alight on the bun table. As she rebolted the side door she realised that she was shaking from head to foot.

The old Charley leaned against the wall.

"Them Bucks," he said. "Wild and wicked they is and wild and wicked they'll remain. But they'll be wet and wicked afore they comes to theirselves, what with the moon gone and their lanterns broke and they all acursing and afighting each other."

His small red face, with its button nose, was suddenly full of twinkling satisfaction.

"They hunts us Charleys and they harries us Charleys but tonight they'll be fair drownded," he said.

He took off his wet hat and seemed to hesitate. "You done well here, Miss Bet," he said. "You done very well. There'll be no change in what's acoming but that's as it should be." And you've afound yourself, Miss Bet. That's clear enough. Now see as you don't alose yourself again."

He gave a little bow. "Good morning to you, Miss Bet," he said and put on his hat.

Betony let him out of the main door. As she relocked it she heard his voice in the empty street. "A dark and rainy morning. All's well!"

In Alexander's study the two letters lay on the table, under the edge of the sketch book. A scattering of rain had driven in wetting the book, and Betony closed the windows and dried it with a screw of paper. Then she took the letters and crept up to her garret.

She had expected to lie awake for the rest of the night, but she fell asleep at once.

28

Letter from Katharine

It was Mrs Rock who woke Betony. The house-keeper was white-faced, and the candle shook in her hand.

"Katharine is not in my parlour," she said. "She has not slept on the sofa. Did you hear anything in the night? I am near distracted with anxiety."

"Katharine's gone," said Betony. "But everything will be all right. I've a letter for you."

She fumbled under her pillow. "Here it is," she said.

Mrs Rock put down her candle and unfolded the paper. And Betony, seeing her look of desperation and fear, said quickly, "You needn't worry, Katharine will be safe with Alexander."

"Alexander?" said Mrs Rock.

"Read your letter," said Betony.

But Mrs Rock seemed to have great difficulty in reading the small, neat handwriting.

"You needn't worry," said Betony again.

"Katharine thanks me for my concern for her," said Mrs Rock at last. "She tells me that she has known Alexander for years. She is gone, and will not return. So all my bitter years of waiting are of no account."

"You should be glad that Katharine's happy," said Betony quickly. "And you should be glad that Alexander—"

"Glad?" said Mrs Rock. "When Katharine should be here with me, her mother? How is it that you had Katharine's letter? You must have known—"

"Yes," said Betony.

"Then why did you not come to me?" cried Mrs Rock. "Had I not a right to be told? Have you no feeling? Annie is right. You are wicked. Wicked! Wicked! Why did you not come to me?"

"I gave two promises," said Betony. "One to you and one to Alexander. And I kept those promises."

"But you must know where Katharine is now?" said Mrs Rock. "And you will tell me instantly. I am her mother, and have a right to be told. Tell me."

"I don't know," said Betony. "But when Katharine and Alexander are married they will return to the village."

"So Katharine will be thrust up out of her station and every evil will follow," said Mrs Rock.

Her face had sharpened and she looked pinched and old.

"It is the one thing that I dreaded above all others," she said. "Katharine's history will be what mine has been – loss and unending grief, hardship and pain."

"Nonsense!" said Betony. "Nonsense!"

"You have too bold a tongue," said Mrs Rock. "And you will oblige me by recollecting that you are—"

"I'm recollecting that I'm myself and *not* Betsy," said Betony. "And now I'm speaking as myself. You've tried to take charge of Katharine's life and fit it into your plans. But Katharine's life is her own and she's taken charge of it. I suppose, at one time or another, we all have to do that."

"The Mistress too, had plans," said Mrs Rock. "*Mon Dieu!* She will be beside herself with rage. And when she discovers that I am Katharine's mother she will turn me out in the street."

"Only *I* know that you are Katharine's mother," said Betony. "And there's no need to tell anyone else – if you don't want to."

"No," said Mrs Rock slowly. "No, there is no need. I must keep my place. Here, at least, I have a position and some authority. And my own fire. I cannot walk the streets again in search of work. And I may still be of some use to Katharine."

"I must get up now," said Betony. "I've a letter to deliver to Mr Dovewood. I suppose he's down in the bakehouse with his men?"

"I believe so," said Mrs Rock. "I cannot tell what this day will bring, but you must attend the Reading. Discipline and order must be preserved — as far as is possible. After the Reading, you will be at liberty to go. You will come to my parlour at ten o'clock, to receive your wages."

She lighted Betony's candle from her own. "I will tell Annie that you are awake," she said. "Now give me the letter for the Master and I will take it to him. He had best have it at once. I only trust he may keep the news from the Mistress for a few more hours."

Betony gave her the letter. And looking across the wavering candle flame she saw that Mrs Rock had regained her composure, the hard, desolate composure of despair.

29

Letter from Alexander

The Reading began as usual.

"Now where is the Master?" said Mrs Dovewood. And the boy was sent running to the bakehouse.

Mrs Dovewood was wearing a new morning cap trimmed with bunched pink ribbons. She leaned forward, resting her head on her hand, and she crossed out a single word and inserted another.

"Today my tale draws to an end," she said. "Today my labours are completed."

"How happy you must be, Madam," said Annie softly. "How very happy."

Mrs Dovewood smiled. And Betony, watching her, thought that she was, indeed, like some posturing but deadly monster, whose egotism and iron will had distorted those lives that touched her own.

Then the boy came flying back.

The Master, he said, had been gone out since six o'clock that morning.

"We shall not wait for him then," said Mrs Dovewood. "The loss will be his." And she began to read.

But Betony made no attempt to listen. Soon, she thought, I shall be home. Soon! Soon! Soon!

Mrs Dovewood's performance continued. Sometimes she raised her voice and sometimes dropped it to a dramatic whisper. She sighed, gesticulated, and once pointed heavenwards.

Then, suddenly, the door was flung open and Oliver Dovewood burst into the room. He was still in his hat and greatcoat, and soaked with rain.

"Mr Dovewood, you are interrupting the Reading," said the Mistress.

"Mrs Dovewood, I have news for you," shouted Oliver Dovewood.

Mrs Dovewood put down her papers. She was flushed under her rouge.

"Look at your boots, Mr Dovewood," she said. "You are as muddy as a road sweeper."

"And little wonder," cried Oliver Dovewood. "I have been going up and down, up and down, enquiring at all the coaching offices and – but that's no matter. In short, Mrs Dovewood, I have had a letter, a letter of the utmost importance and interest. No, no! There is no need to send the servants out of the room. Let them hear what I have to say and then there will be no silly whispering and gossip below stairs. My dear Mrs Dovewood, I have had a letter from my son."

"From Alexander?" said Mrs Dovewood. "And what need has he to write when he can speak to you at any time?"

"Aha, my dear, but that is just the point," said Oliver Dovewood. "He cannot speak to me. He is gone."

"Gone?" said Mrs Dovewood. "Well if he is gone I daresay we shall do well enough without him. Where is he gone?"

"That is just what I have been endeavouring to discover," said Oliver Dovewood. "He is gone off with a country miss, to be married. He writes that he has been acquainted with her for a number of years."

"Now that, indeed, is news!" cried Mrs Dovewood. "Have I not told you a thousand times that Alexander's repeated visits to the country could mean but one thing – that he had met some young lady who had taken his fancy? But who is the girl? Has her family forbid the match that Alexander must run off with his charmer? A secret elopement is romantic enough, Mr Dovewood, but it is foolhardy, extremely foolhardy. If the young lady's parents will not be reconciled with her she may discover that she is penniless. And then—"

"She has no parents," said Oliver Dovewood.

"She has a guardian then?" said Mrs Dovewood. "Now that is no bad thing provided that her fortune has been properly cared for."

"She has no guardian," said Oliver Dovewood. "And she has no fortune. Not a penny. But from what Alexander writes she is a paragon of beauty, sweetness and modesty."

Mrs Dovewood rose to her feet, and her voice was sharp with anger. "Give me the letter," she cried. "Give it to me this instant. Alexander must be brought back. Are you mad, Mr Dovewood, that you stand there doing nothing? No parents! No fortune! The matter must be hushed up. Give me the letter."

"The letter was addressed to me," said Oliver Dovewood. "And as to being mad – why, I believe I am no madder than I was yesterday. It is too late to bring Alexander back. Nor would I if I could. But he should have trusted me. I was not like to have proved a hard father."

"I will take the carriage and go after him myself," cried Mrs Dovewood. "I will force him to return. I will send the girl packing."

"My dear Madam, you will do nothing of the sort," said Oliver Dovewood. "A young fellow, with a mind of his own, must be permitted to choose his own wife. And I cannot find it in my heart to blame the girl for attaching herself to Alexander. I have always thought him the most agreeable son that any man could have. But he should have trusted me. I would have made them such a cake for the wedding as would have astonished all London."

"Alexander is unworthy of his name," cried Mrs Dovewood. "He is a traitor to the family. You will not see him again, Mr Dovewood. You will cast him off. He is no true Dovewood."

"Fiddlesticks!" said Oliver Dovewood. "I say fiddlesticks, Mrs Dovewood. I say stuff and nonsense! It appears that you have forgot one small matter – that Alexander is *my* son. He is not yours, Mrs Dovewood, and you will oblige me by remembering that. He writes that he and his bride, Katharine, will return to the village, where she has spent most of her life, as soon as they are married. And there I shall visit them at the earliest possible moment. And you may come with me or not, Madam, as you please."

"I will never see him again," shrieked Mrs Dovewood. "And I will never hear him spoke of." She had begun to pace round the table, wringing her hands and tossing her head. "I will strike him from my memory."

"Then I must go alone," said Oliver Dovewood. "Now do calm yourself, Mrs Dovewood. This is no occasion to enact a tragedy."

But Mrs Dovewood clutched at her heart and groaned. She burst into peals of high-pitched laughter, flung up her arms and ended by sweeping all the papers and pens off the table. Then she snatched at her morning cap and stamped on it.

"Oh, my poor mistress!" cried Annie. "Her plans have all been set at nought. Oh, Madam, your new cap!"

"Fetch some cold water, girl, and throw it in your mistress's face," said Oliver Dovewood. He seemed curiously unperturbed and Betony realised, suddenly, that Mrs Dovewood was merely giving another performance. The Mistress was not the woman to be caught up in genuine hysteria.

"Cold water!" roared Oliver Dovewood. "Fetch a bucket full."

Mrs Dovewood sank, with a heart-rending moan, into her chair and covered her face with her hands.

"You may fetch my smelling-salts, Annie," she said. "I shall retire to my bed when – when – I have the power to stand."

"And I must return to the bakehouse," said Oliver Dovewood.

"The Reading is over," said Mrs Rock. "And there is work to be done."

Linaria or Toadflax

30

Wages

Betony climbed the stairs to her garret. She changed into her own clothes, left those she had been wearing folded on the chair, and repacked the servant's box. She turned the straw mattress and set the sheets aside. Then she put on her cloak.

She looked round the garret and could think of nothing more to do. It was still too early for the visit to Mrs Rock's parlour so she sat down on the bed.

She was going home. And, already, the black garret, with its view of smoking chimneys and the text on the wall, had become an alien place in which she simply waited.

But I must say goodbye to Clara, she thought. She was

conscious of a dream-like sense of release, but conscious, too, of Alexander's empty study below.

I shall see him again, sometime, she thought. It doesn't really matter when. I shall certainly see him.

Then she heard Clara's voice on the stairs.

> "*The sojer, tired of war's alarms*
> *For-swears the clang o' hostile arms*
> *And scorns the spear—*"

There was a knock on the door and Clara burst into the room. "Well, there's the Missus safe behind her bed curtains," she said, "and Annie dancing attendance on her, with warming-pans, and smelling-salts. Now you're a sly one, Bet. Oh, you're a sly one."

She plumped down on the bed beside Betony. "There's Mrs Rock have just tell me as you've give warning and is going home today," she said, "and you never let out a single word to me, Bet. I'll miss you, that I will. You're the strangest Betsy as ever I worked with but you got a kind heart and I'll miss you."

Betony smiled. "I don't think *you'll* be here much longer," she said.

"No more do I," said Clara. "Listen, Bet! D'you know what I just found, tied to the knocker on the airy door? A new dream book, Bet, all wrap up neat in paper and having *Miss Clara* wrote on it. And it's from my sojer."

"So he knew you'd lost the other dream book," said Betony.

Clara giggled. "He knew, Bet, because I tell him," she said. "It were when I were last cleaning me front windows and he come by. And he say to me as he hopes the Missus don't forbid followers in dreams. And he say as he's been calling on me, regular in his dreams, and he hopes he figures in mine. And I laughs, Bet, and say as I don't doubt the Missus would put a stop to it if she could, but then, I says, I don't know as I'll be here for ever. And he say, No, dammit, he'll see as I isn't. Lord, Bet, there's that Annie calling. She's in as wicked a temper this morning as ever I seen, and muttering to herself about the Devil taking care of his own. Lord, Bet, I'll have to go."

She flung her arms round Betony. "I'll miss you, Bet," she said again. "I'll miss you. Goodbye, Bet."

Then she was gone.

It was three minutes to ten.

Betony slipped down the stairs to Mrs Rock's parlour. The room was empty but a single gold sovereign and a few smaller coins were spread out on the table.

My wages, thought Betony. The first money I've ever earned.

Mrs Rock came in quickly and shut the door behind her.

"Well," she said. "There is the money that you are entitled to. You had best put it in your purse at once. You may be assured that I shall not call on you again."

"I know," said Betony.

"You have done well enough," said Mrs Rock. "But you should learn to curb your tongue."

"I don't think I want the money," said Betony. "Will you give it to the children – the poor ones that come into the shop for halfpenny buns?"

"I have no patience with improvidence," said Mrs Rock. "Put the money in your purse."

"Give it to the children," said Betony. "Now I must go home."

"I will light a pastille then," said Mrs Rock. Her hand shook as she lifted the china cottage off the mantelpiece.

"Alexander and Katharine are gone off," she said slowly. "But he may change his mind. He may ruin her and then desert her. He may—"

"You should know Alexander better than that," said Betony.

"I know nothing," said Mrs Rock. "The young Master has not confided in me for years and Katharine has deceived me."

"In both cases it was largely your fault," said Betony. "Now listen! You've never asked my name, but it seems that I must tell you. I'm like Katharine. And my name is Dovewood. Betony Dovewood. Now do you understand? I'm a Dovewood and I have *the other face*."

The china cottage slipped from Mrs Rock's hand and fell to the carpet.

"*Mon Dieu!*" she said. "I never guessed. How could I have guessed? How could I? And you have the look of Katharine. So all may yet be well for Katharine. But not for me – not for me."

She pressed her clenched hands on her heart.

"Katharine will become the young Mistress," she said. "And I shall hold my tongue. Well, I still have my own fire. And if my heart breaks it's no great matter."

Betony stooped and picked up the cottage. A crack, like a flash of lightning, ran down through the painted roses and morning glories.

"I beg your pardon, Miss Dovewood, for not recognising that you belonged to the Master's family," said Mrs Rock. "I understood, at once, that you came from – from – a great way off. But I did not put two and two together."

She curtsied.

"I will give the money to the children," she said. "I am greatly obliged to you, Miss Dovewood. You will find the pastilles in the drawer of the table. Now I beg that you will excuse me. I have to inspect the bedrooms."

She curtsied again. "Good morning, Miss Dovewood."

31

The Bell

Betony replaced the china cottage on its green plinth. Then, slowly, a sense of irrevocable disaster, followed by a numbing, desperate fear took hold of her.

Now that the crack belonged to both times, the past and her own time, she would never get home.

Her hands were icy, under her cloak, and she could feel the beating of her heart.

Alexander has gone, she thought, and I can't stay in this house. But where can I go? The world outside the windows is not mine. If I am lost in it, with no hope of finding my way back to my own world, what will happen to me?

There was the usual shouting in the street below, the usual creaking of carts and clatter of horses. She heard the distant cry of the old clothes man. She had begun to tremble. This dreadful cold terror was something that she had never experienced before.

I was a kind of ghost when I went to Number 26, thought Betony, and I found that I was Betony Dovewood *here*, while I played Betsy. I suppose Alexander helped me. I should have liked to tell Spurrey about it, but I can't even send him a message. I shall never see him again. Or Linny, or Jacob. They'll never know what has happened to me. And Linny will think I've broken my promise.

She shut her eyes. The pain was almost more than she could bear.

Linny will miss me, she thought. And so will Spurrey.

But they'll forget me in the end. And Jacob will stop asking, "Is B-B-Betony back yet?" They'll go on leading their own lives in their own time, while I am here, a ghost again, caught in the wrong time for ever and ever. If only I could have explained to Linny—

She pulled her cloak round her.

I must go, she thought. I must go. I mustn't be found here. Now that I can never get back . . . never get back . . .

The words seemed to echo and re-echo in her mind like a bell, a cruel, clanging bell.

Never get back! . . . Never get back! . . .

But faintly, somewhere, a real bell was ringing, on and on and on. And suddenly, through the noises of the street, she heard Linny's voice, infinitely far off but clear.

"Hasn't Betony come yet? She meant to come today. She won't mind now if I call her. Betony! Betony! Betony! It's time you came back. Betony! Betony! BETONY!"

32

Letter from Aunt May

The bell was still ringing as Betony slipped into the shop.

"So there you are!" cried Linny. "I was afraid you wouldn't come. I was afraid—" She rushed at Betony and kissed her. "You've been gone a terribly long time," she cried. "And you didn't even send us a postcard."

"I'm glad you're back," said Spurrey. "Very glad."

"I went out to do the Saturday shopping," said Linny. "And I said to myself: if Betony isn't there when I get back I shall shout and shout. And you weren't. So I did. I shouted and shouted. And here you are!"

"How did you know I meant to come today?" asked Betony.

Linny looked at her uncertainly.

"Well," she said, "I – I had a dream. At least I think it was a dream. And you were standing near some door, and it was night. And you said that you were coming today. And there was a cloud over the moon. And – and I think that it was raining. I told Spurrey that you'd be back today. And I told Gerard. And I told Jacob."

"Jacob?" said Betony.

"He's painting the drawing-room," said Linny. "Oh, I *am* glad you've come back. I don't want you ever to go to that place again."

"I won't," said Betony. "I can't."

She looked at Linny.

"So it wasn't the crack after all," said Betony. "It was

you who brought me back. And you've done it three times."

"Yes," said Linny. "But I like you, that's why. Here's Gerard. I think I'll just run upstairs and tell Jacob you've come."

Betony looked round. Nothing in the shop had changed. There were still boxes everywhere.

"So you're back," said Gerard. "How was the job?"

"Hard work," said Betony.

"In that note you left Spurrey you never told him what the job was," said Gerard, and added, "You've changed, you know."

"Yes," said Betony.

Then Jacob appeared behind the counter, with Linny behind him.

"Hallo B-Betony," he said. "I'm glad you're home at last."

"So am I," said Betony.

"There's a letter for you," said Gerard. "It was registered and came four days ago. It's downstairs on the mantelpiece. I'm afraid it's from the Aunts."

"I'd almost forgotten them," said Betony slowly. "I suppose I wanted to forget them. It's still only February. I don't have to go back yet."

"I'll fetch the letter," said Gerard.

Dear Betony, wrote Aunt May. *You have left us in the lurch for quite long enough. It is high time that you returned to Dovewood House. The doctor has always been a fool and you must pull yourself together. The so-called housekeeper left last Thursday, having invaded my room when I was resting and used the most insulting language. As for the gardener – he had taken to coming later and later and has now finally departed. He is no great loss.*

*Your Aunt Maple has been doing the shopping but
refuses to make any attempt to cook hot meals. As you
know I am not, myself, well enough to shop or cook. I
enclose your fare and shall expect to see you on Thursday or Friday of this week. Your Aunt Maple agrees
with me that you must come back at once.*
   Yours,
    May Dovewood.

Betony read the letter twice, once to herself and once
aloud.

"But you won't go, will you?" cried Linny anxiously.
"The Aunts said you could stay here till the middle of
March."

"I don't know what I shall do," said Betony. "Did
anyone tell the Aunts that I wasn't here?"

"I sent a postcard to Dovewood House and said you
were away," said Gerard. "It's about time the Aunts had
a phone."

"Mrs O'Connor is having a holiday," said Linny. "I
must go and make a pudding."

Jacob joined them for lunch. He still appeared melancholy, watchful and curiously diffident.

"I've finished painting our flat," he said, "b-but this
painting b-business is very engrossing and I didn't want
to stop. So I do a b-bit every week-end. What have you
decided about the Aunts?"

"Nothing yet," said Betony. "I need time to think."

"You *have* changed," said Gerard. "Now, since we're
all here, tell us about the job."

"If I do you won't believe me," said Betony. But she
told them.

Spurrey got up and began to pace about the room. The
others listened silently.

"Of course there's a rational explanation," said Gerard

at the end. "I suppose you won't believe me if I assure you that the whole thing was imagination."

"No," said Betony. "I shan't believe you."

"Of course you must have been somewhere, since you weren't here," said Gerard. "But it's clear that your imagination took complete charge of you. What do you say, Spurrey? Alexander and all those other people were simply figments of Betony's imagination. There's no other possible explanation."

"I know that imagination is about the most powerful instrument that man has at his disposal," said Spurrey. "But in this case—"

"You're sitting on the fence as usual, Spurrey," said Gerard. "I suppose you've been doing that all your life."

"Well," said Spurrey. "I've always found the fence the safest place to sit when I was uncertain of the ground on either side of it."

"I *knew* that Betony had gone to the other shop," said Linny. "I knew it all the time. And everything she says is true."

"There's only one rational explanation," said Gerard. "And Betony's got to accept it."

Jacob stood up suddenly.

"Why?" he said. "The only thing that matters is that B-Betony's b-back."

"We're living in the modern world," said Gerard slowly. "You seem to forget that."

"Perhaps not *all* of us are – not *all* the time," said Spurrey.

33

The Sunday Visitors

They had finished breakfast and washed up.

Betony unbolted the shop door and collected the milk-bottles from the step. It was a mild, shining morning and no one was about. Albert Terrace was taking its well-earned Sunday rest and the pale sun glinted on empty pavements.

Betony left the door open and turned to survey the shop.

Yesterday morning, she thought, I attended the Reading. And Mrs Dovewood stamped and screamed and swept all her papers off the table. And now I'm here again . . . But, of course, it wasn't yesterday morning. It was years and years ago.

Curzon peered down from the top of the cupboard, thrust out a tentative paw and then returned to his morning sleep.

"It's all right for you," said Betony. "But I've still to write to the Aunts."

Spurrey appeared behind the counter in his muffler and overcoat, as the hall clock struck half past ten.

"I thought I'd go down to the river," he said. "The ducks will like this weather. And I always enjoy the sun on the water."

"I'm going to finish tidying the cupboard," said Betony. "I'll see to lunch later."

"And your letter?" said Spurrey.

"The post doesn't go till three-thirty,' said Betony. "So I've still a little time."

"That reminds me," said Spurrey. "Mrs O'Connor

sent me a mysterious postcard last week. There were snowdrops on it."

"I shouldn't have thought snowdrops were very mysterious," said Betony.

"It was the other side," said Spurrey. "She said you were a good girl and she hoped your temporary job was satisfactory. Then she said she'd seen how things were and if you couldn't be useful in this world where could you be useful. Now what do you make of that?"

"I don't know," said Betony. "When's Mrs O'Connor coming back?"

"She didn't say," said Spurrey. "But I must admit to a certain – certain – apprehension at the thought of her return. Those boxes are still in the hall."

"I'll try to find room for them in the cupboard," said Betony. "What's in them?"

"Nothing," said Spurrey. "But I could never bring myself to throw them away."

The two remaining high shelves in the cupboard had still to be tidied. Betony fetched the steps. But the shadow of Dovewood House, that place of loneliness and endurance, lay over the bright morning.

I've still a little time, thought Betony. Still a few hours before I need write.

She lifted down piles of old school-books and bundles of receipts, and the five family albums.

Then the bell clanged softly and Jacob appeared.

"I thought you'd be ti-d-dying the cupboard," he said. "I suppose Gerard and Linny are busy with their homework. I usually make coffee on Sunday morning for anyone who wants it. Would you like a cup?"

"It's exactly what I need," said Betony.

Jacob propped himself against the counter. "Have you written to the Aunts yet?" he asked.

"No," said Betony.

"Of course I'm only an outsider," said Jacob, "b-but it seems to me that Spurrey's a b-bit lonely. Of course he wouldn't even hint that he'd like you to stay the full time b-but – b-but he's like the man he painted in the snow, waiting and waiting."

"Yes," said Betony. "But the Aunts are old."

"They're not *so* old," said Jacob. "And it seems to me that they're taking advantage of you."

"Does it?" said Betony. "They gave me a place to live."

"Oh well," said Jacob. "I'll make the coffee."

When he returned, with their two cups, Betony had climbed the steps again.

"It looks as though you could d-do with a b-bit of help," said Jacob.

"I could," said Betony. "But I'll drink my coffee first." After that they worked together.

"There are only a few more things up here on the final shelf," said Betony at last. "There's a collection of vases and a package done up in newspaper, and—"

The bell clanged violently and the shop door was flung open. Jacob hurried forward.

"I'm afraid the shop's closed," he said.

"The shop is obviously *not* closed," said Aunt May. "Who are you? And where's Spurrey? Has Betony—?"

She advanced into the shop with Aunt Maple behind her.

"Oh, there you are, Betony," she said. "What on earth are you doing on those steps? You look like a monkey up a stick. Come down at once."

Aunt Maple pushed forward. "We've a car outside and it can't be kept waiting," she said. "We'll take you back with us."

Betony looked down. And it seemed to her that she was seeing the Aunts for the first time.

Away from Dovewood House they appeared strangely diminished – two eccentric, ageing women who had quarrelled with each other all their lives, and had made no concessions to anyone. Aunt May, mountainous, slow-moving and arrogant, stood peering about her. Her white hair straggled from under her shapeless hat and she wore an ancient fur coat.

Aunt Maple was in emerald green, with a red and yellow scarf draped over her fiery hair.

"Well?" said Aunt May. "What are you staring at? Come down off those ridiculous steps and go and fetch Spurrey. Then collect your things."

"Spurrey's gone down to the river," said Betony.

"And who is this extraordinary-looking youth?"

"Jacob's a friend," said Betony. "Spurrey's friend and ours. And this isn't Dovewood House, Aunt May, it's Spurrey's shop."

Aunt May subsided majestically on to the chair by the counter.

"And the shop hasn't changed," she said. "It was always a disgrace. Well? What are you waiting for?"

"I'm not coming back with you now," said Betony. "I can't go away without a word to Spurrey. I'll let you know when to expect me back at Dovewood House."

"I've no intention of leaving without you," said Aunt May. "You're behaving like a naughty child. You don't seem yourself."

"Don't I?" said Betony. "I feel more myself now than I've ever felt before."

"I'll fetch another chair," said Jacob and vanished behind the wardrobe.

"You'll have to explain a great deal, Betony," said Aunt Maple. "You'll have to explain where you've been and what you've been doing. But that can wait, and the car can't. Will you come down off those steps!"

"No," said Betony. "Not until I've said what I want to say."

There was a deathly silence. It was the first time in her life she had dared to defy the Aunts.

Jacob returned with the chair and Aunt Maple sat down.

"Now please listen," said Betony. "I'll come back to Dovewood House in a day or two. And I'll look after you as well as I can because you took me in, and because you're getting old. But I shall expect a month's holiday every year so that I can come to see Spurrey. And you'll have to learn to talk to each other again because I shan't carry any more messages."

She hesitated.

"Can't you *see* how you're wasting your lives?" she said. "Can't you *see*?"

Aunt May began to tap on the counter; Aunt Maple jerked to her feet.

"Your stay here has hardly improved you, Betony," she said. "You seem very quickly to have forgotten what you owe us. You've neither personality nor artistic gifts, like the true Dovewoods. And now it appears that you lack gratitude." She rounded suddenly on Jacob. "This is a family discussion," she said. "Will you kindly go home. You're in the way."

"Please stay," said Betony quickly. "I should like you to stay."

There was another silence.

Aunt May was still tapping on the counter.

"I must warn you, Betony," she said at last. "I must warn you—"

"There is still Dovewood House," said Aunt Maple.

"Leave Dovewood House out of the discussion," said Aunt May sharply. "There is no need to mention Dovewood House. I say there is no need."

"I shall mention anything I choose," said Aunt Maple. "It is not for you to dictate, May. You have been dictating to people all your life but I will *not* put up with it."

"I say that this is not the time to speak of Dovewood House," said Aunt May. "I am still alive and relatively well. And so – presumably – are you. I say that this is *not* the time."

"I consider that it *is* the time," said Aunt Maple. "Because unless Betony returns with us now—"

"You are a fool, Maple," said Aunt May. "A damned fool! But then you always were. Will you never learn to leave well alone?"

"Unless Betony returns with us now, I shall take steps," said Aunt Maple. "I shall see to it, May, I shall see to it. Make no mistake. My half of Dovewood House will pass into other hands. But you, of course must do as you please – as you've been doing all your life, without the smallest reference to my feelings, or anyone else's."

Betony looked down at them. "Are you saying that you intended me to inherit Dovewood House?" she asked.

"That is precisely what I *am* saying," said Aunt Maple. "But unless you return with us now—"

"I don't want Dovewood House," said Betony. "And I shall never want it. I hate it."

"Three cheers!" muttered Jacob.

Aunt May rose to her feet clutching her fur coat. She was slightly flushed and looked extraordinarily like Mrs Dovewood. For one brief instant Betony feared that Aunt May was going to snatch off her brown hat and stamp on it. Instead she sat down again.

"The letters," she said. "We've forgotten the letters, Maple."

"Of course," said Aunt Maple. "The letters."

"It appears that in one thing, at least, we are fortunate," said Aunt May. "Yes, I believe that we are very fortunate – in that we are not entirely dependent on Betony. You have the letters, Maple?"

"Yes," said Aunt Maple and began to fumble in her handbag.

"Mrs O's a sensible woman," said Aunt May. "She'll be willing enough to stand in. And her nursing experience will be particularly useful to me. There's no reason why we shouldn't offer her a room. If she lives in the house – Have you found those letters, Maple?"

"Here they are," said Aunt Maple.

"I shall be interested to hear what she writes to Betony," said Aunt May. "Give the girl her letter. We'll leave Spurrey's on the counter."

Betony sat down on the top of the steps with the letter. It was a thick package and she was bewildered.

"We've stolen a march on Spurrey," said Aunt May. "He'll have to get along as best he can. Well, read your letter."

Betony tore open the envelope.

34

Letter from Mrs O'Connor

Dear Betony, wrote Mrs O'Connor. *I don't know whether you're back yet at 26, but the Dragons will deliver this letter. It makes me laugh to think of them handing it over. It really makes me laugh. You could have knocked me down with a feather when I heard you'd taken a job, I mean I didn't think you'd that much enterprise, or energy. Well what I want to say is don't come back. It's all wrong you in that great museum of a place with those two selfish old specimens like mummies wrapped up in themselves, and not a clue as to what's going on outside. You see I couldn't get you out of my mind so I thought I'd have a bit of a holiday, while Linny and Gerard were still with Mr Spurrey. Well, I asked about trains, packed a bag and paid a visit to Dovewood House. When I got there I rang the bell and said I'd come to talk about you.*

Miss Maple let me in and started off with complaints before the door was shut. And then I had to see the family photos and what she'd been doing to them. And if you ask me she's made them look like a lot of Punch and Judys. Macaber, I call it, but I didn't say so.

Well, then, Miss May came downstairs to see who'd arrived, having heard the bell and our voices. She was in an old brown hat and woollen bed socks. And Miss Maple went and looked out of the window. So then I really understood why you'd appeared like a half-drowned ghost when I first saw you. Them not talking to each other I mean. So don't you dare come back.

Well, then Miss May took me up to her room and told me about her health and the Fire of Life that had to be kept alight. And I said if you keep stoking a fire with the wrong fuel you'll end by putting the fire out. And you should have seen her face, especially when I said I'd had years of nursing experience. Well, then I had to hear for the second time about the rude housekeeper and the gardener who'd come late. And I said could I go and look at the garden. And then I knew like a flash of lightning what I was going to do. I always say if you can't be useful in this world where can you be useful? And I'm what you might call a free agent.

Well, I went back into the house and said I'd take over the garden. I said I'd expect the proper wages and wanted the wild part at the end for myself. And they agreed, first Miss May and then Miss Maple. And I knew what they were thinking.

I know their sort and they were thinking that I was a treasure (and I'll not say I'm not), and they were thinking that I'd be useful as Head Nurse and Bottle-washer if ever the need arose. Well, they've got another think coming.

But don't you dare come back.

It'll be good for them to do a bit in the house for themselves. Miss May has got to be got up and about. I'll see they get help and keep an eye on them but I'll not do a stroke more than I've agreed to do. What will happen is that they'll gang up against me when they find I'm up to their little tricks. They'll begin to complain about me to each other and that'll get them talking. It'll be two against one but I've always enjoyed a fight. And they won't sack me because I'm reliable. And when all the teething troubles are ironed out they'll be eating out of my hand.

145

I saw how Mr Spurrey took to you. You may even be able to make a go of the shop, although I doubt it. But do see he doesn't go out in his slippers. I've written him a note and you can tell him the rest. He won't mind that I haven't given proper notice. He was always as easy-going as a lamb except when he was as obstinate as a mule. Do get him to move those boxes in the hall.

Well, I'm in a bed-sitter but shall try for a flat. The Dragons think you're coming back, but a few more years with them and they'll have drained all the life out of you. It's like Come and Sit on My Chair which is a game kids play at parties in case you don't know. You look as though you've never been to a party in your life. The kids keep changing chairs until they find the right one. Well that's all for now.

I've started a compost heap and done a bit of digging. It's lovely to be able to look a seed catalogue in the face. I've been collecting them for years.

Please give my respects to Mr Spurrey. I hope he's got all those snow storms out of his system. Tell him to paint a nice garden.

It's funny how things happen. I shall have a sundial in my bit of garden. They used to tell the time by them in the old days. I like to think of that. I'll come in and see you all when I collect my bits and pieces.

Well, goodbye for now,
  Yours sincerely,
    Mrs O'Connor
P.S. I'll see about sending your things but you seem to have precious little. I shall plant pansies round the sundial.
    Mrs O'C.

"Mrs O'Connor appears to have written at extraordinary length," said Aunt May. "What does she say?"

"She thinks she'll have pansies round her sundial," said Betony.

Then the shop bell clanged and in came Spurrey. "I forgot my watch," he said, "And—" he stopped.

"Well, Spurrey?" said Aunt May.

"You've aged, Spurrey," said Aunt Maple. "You should wear brighter colours."

"You must forgive me if I seem somewhat taken aback," said Spurrey. "I did not expect—"

"I must say, Spurrey, you've certainly not worn well," said Aunt May. "You should eat more. One has to stoke the Fire of Life – but always, of course, with the proper fuel."

"It's a good many years, since we last met," said Spurrey mildly. "Is this a social call or have you come for some particular purpose?"

"We shouldn't be here if we hadn't come for a particular purpose," said Aunt Maple.

"We came to fetch Betony – if she were here," said Aunt May. "But in the circumstances—"

"Ingratitude is something that I cannot –will not – live with," said Aunt Maple. "We've agreed that Betony had best go her own way."

"Good," said Spurrey. "I've always believed that *that* was the best way to go."

"It's precisely what you would believe," said Aunt May. "And look where it's led you. Here's a note from Mrs O'Connor. You'd better open it at once."

"An admirable woman," said Spurrey, "but how is it—?" He looked down at the envelope.

"But Mrs O'Connor's on holiday," he said.

"You'd better read her letter," said Aunt Maple. "For once we agree, Spurrey. Mrs O'Connor's an admirable woman and I imagine you've never appreciated her."

"I've had a letter too," said Betony quickly. "Mrs O'Connor isn't coming back."

"Aaah!" said Spurrey. "Of course she always wanted a garden."

He read his letter.

"Brief and to the point," he said. "She's got a garden."

"We believe that we can induce Mrs O'Connor to take rather more than the garden into her charge," said Aunt May.

"Induce?" said Spurrey.

"Persuade," said Aunt Maple.

"I don't doubt," said Spurrey, "that in a few years the Dovewood garden will rival the Garden of Eden. But as to inducing, or persuading, Mrs O'Connor to do anything she doesn't want to do—"

"We shall see," said Aunt May. "We shall see."

"I believe you will," said Spurrey.

"I'll fetch the money you sent me for the fare," said Betony.

The china cottage still stood on the bedside table. Betony stared down at it. I suppose the real magic lies in people themselves, she thought. They're extraordinary and unpredictable.

She was aware of relief, of huge, overwhelming relief. She was aware, too, of joy but hesitated to recognise it for what is was.

I wish I could talk to Alexander, she thought. He'd understand. He believed in miracles. I wish he could send me a postcard from his sweet grove.

She turned to go and caught a glimpse of her face in the mirror. She was smiling.

Of course Gerard would say that a figment of the imagination couldn't be expected to understand anything, she thought. Or send a postcard.

As she crossed the hall she heard Linny's voice in the shop.

"You're the Aunts, aren't you? I thought you were. I said to Gerard, 'I'm sure it's the Aunts because I can smell mothballs.' Well, if you've come for Betony, you can't have her. You said she could stay till the middle of March so you'd better go away again."

"It's all right," said Betony. "I'm not going back to Dovewood House."

"Not ever?" cried Linny. "Do you mean—?"

"Yes," said Betony. "That's what I mean."

"Oh!" cried Linny. "Oh, I *am* glad! Oh, I could dance and sing! Oh, I could stand on my head for joy! Oh, it's fantastic!"

She flung her arms round Betony.

"I said to Gerard, 'If I can get up the stairs before the clock strikes twelve – then the Aunts will go away,' and Gerard said, 'You're taking a big risk. If the Aunts are in the shop they'll gobble you up,' and I said, 'I don't care. I've got to save Betony. I'm going to rush.' And Gerard said, 'If you'll wait a moment' – But I couldn't. And there's the clock striking now."

"I believe, May, the car has been kept outside long enough," said Aunt Maple.

Aunt May rose majestically. "There's no need to see us to the door, Spurrey," she said. "If you end in the bankruptcy court don't expect us to assist you. You were always a fool and Betony takes after you."

They had gone.

Betony looked across at Spurrey.

"Is it all right if I stay?" she asked.

"Well," said Spurrey. "There are still those boxes in the hall, I don't feel that I can ever cope with them alone."

* * *

149

They had finished lunch.

"What about the cupboard?" said Jacob. "Let's get it done."

"There's not much to do now," said Betony.

Curzon peered down at her as she climbed the steps. He thrust out an amiable paw and left it hanging over the edge.

"He's getting almost human," said Jacob.

"There's only the newspaper package," said Betony. "I'd better just see what's in it."

"It looks like a b-book," said Jacob.

"It is a book," said Betony. "A sketchbook."

The newspaper wrapping slipped to the floor.

"Well?" said Jacob. "You – you look a b-bit queer. Are you all right?"

Betony climbed down and carried the book to the counter.

"The pages are stuck together," she said. "I ought to have thought to dry the edges. Have you a penknife?"

Jacob fumbled in his pocket.

"Yes," he said. "Wait while I open it."

Betony began carefully separating the pages. Her hands were shaking.

"The rain came through the window," she said. "Luckily only the edges are spoilt. They seem to have been loosened once, and then they stuck again. Look! Here's a wild strawberry plant. And here's cinquefoil. I must find the groundsel page. It was the only page I ever saw."

"Is it Alexander's book?" asked Jacob.

"Yes," said Betony. She found the groundsel page and found, too, a slip of paper that had marked the place.

There was a note on the paper in Alexander's curling, exquisite handwriting—

For Betony Dovewood,
  (when she arrives)
This collection of Common Flowers drawn after
Nature, from her most obliged and affectionate Cousin,
  Alexander Dovewood

"It's a pity to d-drip tears on Alexander's message," said Jacob.

"He won't mind," said Betony. "I think they're tears of joy."

Groundsel